CORRUPTIBLE

NATASHA KNIGHT

Copyright © 2017 by Natasha Knight

All rights reserved.

No part of this book may be reproduced in any form or by any electronic or mechanical means, including information storage and retrieval systems, without written permission from the author, except for the use of brief quotations in a book review.

Corruptible was originally published under the title Disgraced.

Click here to sign up for Natasha's newsletter to receive new release news and updates!

1

DAMON

I knew it was her the moment I heard the music.

I stepped in through the nondescript door of Club Carmen. A woman giggled, stumbled through a curtain knocking her shoulder into me on her way out. She bounced off me but I caught her before she fell.

She turned big, drunk eyes up to mine, opened her mouth to apologize, and, at the urging of her friend, slipped past.

"Damon?" Stephanie, the woman I'd come with, called my name. She watched me from the coat check while I stood distracted by that piano.

I smiled and turned to her, wondering what the hell I was doing. Why I'd agreed to bring her here after a business dinner that had already lasted too long. Gavin, my dean at seminary, had arranged the meeting. We needed the funding, and it was my job to ensure we received it.

I helped her with her coat before sliding mine off and handing both to the girl behind the counter. Taking our ticket, I led Stephanie to the next room, a richly decorated space that would fit better in a centuries-old palace in France than in the basement level of a much younger building in Manhattan.

My gaze wandered to the room where the piano music came from. That sound felt familiar. I couldn't place it, but I knew it. Not the piece itself, but the pianist. Didn't every musician have their own signature sound? Or had I just subconsciously memorized hers?

I shook my head to clear it. It wasn't possible it was her. She wasn't here. Not in New York City. Not in this club.

Club Carmen seemed to be made up of a series of rooms off one central, larger space. We entered the one where the grand piano stood beneath the vaulted, frescoed ceiling. Two Greek gods stood on either side of it. It looked as though those gods held up the walls of the building itself. As though without them, they could come crashing down at any moment.

The girl sat beneath those gods behind the piano, illuminated by a soft spotlight, her gaze on the keys. My attention was immediately drawn to her. A strange sensation made its way through me as I looked at her.

"You're going to love this place." Stephanie said.

It took me a moment to process her words, and her deep sigh told me she was annoyed by my lack of attention.

"I already do." I gestured toward an empty table.

It felt surreal, like the music and the lights and maybe the bottle of wine we'd consumed with dinner had been laced with something more, something illicit. Something erotic and forbidden.

Forbidden to me.

As Stephanie looked around for a waitress, I watched the girl. It couldn't be her, though. She was in Chicago. Studying. She couldn't be playing piano at Club Carmen on a Friday night.

Her fingers worked furiously over the keyboard, her concentration intense. Tattoos covered the whole of one arm and shoulder decorating every inch of skin exposed by the little black dress she wore.

Not her. Lina didn't have a single tattoo.

"Finally," Stephanie muttered as a waitress approached.

"Can I get you a drink?" the waitress asked.

"A vodka martini," Stephanie replied.

"I'll have a whiskey neat."

"Be right back."

I met Stephanie's gaze. Seductive. She had expectations for tonight. Expectations I thought I'd checked over the last three days I'd had to spend with her. I'd tolerated it at first. Now I was irritated. I wasn't here to fuck her.

When the waitress returned with our drinks, I asked her if she knew the pianist's name. She glanced over her shoulder and smiled.

"She's amazing, isn't she?"

"She is."

"Kat something. I don't know her last name. I can ask if you like?"

Stephanie shifted her gaze from me to the girl behind the piano and back, taking the measure of what I assumed she considered her competition.

It reminded me of the reason I'd been banished to this city in the first place. To figure out what I wanted, where I belonged. Who the hell I was.

I shook my head. Not the time for those thoughts.

"No," I said to the waitress. "That's all right. I thought it was someone else."

I thought it was Lina.

I'd listened to Lina play countless times when she'd lived with Raphael and Sofia. But I hadn't heard from her in the last two years. She'd disappeared from my life as effectively as I'd disappeared from hers.

As soon as the waitress left, Stephanie spoke. "Do you know her or something?"

She didn't hide her annoyance well. An edge sharpened her tone. Stephanie's father had been a great supporter of St. Mark's Seminary. He'd attended it in his younger years, and even though he'd chosen a life outside the church, he'd always given generously to help keep it running.

As his only child, Stephanie had inherited the family fortune. I'd been sent to ensure those donations would keep coming. Well, that was one of the reasons.

"No. I thought she looked familiar, but I was mistaken."

"The way you were looking at her, I thought you did." She smiled, leaned toward me. "What a waste it will be."

"What will be?"

"You're too young and handsome to devote your life to the church. I'm sure I'm not the first woman to tell you that."

I felt her hand at my knee but shifted my position and cleared my throat.

"No, actually. You're the first," I said, finishing my drink, finished with Stephanie. I set my glass down. "You realize nothing is going to happen between us," I said bluntly because people like Stephanie needed blunt.

"I don't know what you mean, Damon."

"You are aware that I haven't left the seminary. I'm here as a representative of it."

"I have no idea what you're talking about." She straightened, glanced around the room.

"No?" I asked, leaning toward her.

She leaned in too, encouraged, perhaps. Her gaze roamed over my face, lingering at my mouth before returning to my eyes.

"When Father Gavin set up this meeting, I was expecting to meet a very different man."

"Different?" I raised my eyebrows.

She shrugged a shoulder. "Please, Damon, you're not stupid. And you forget, I know Gavin. I know how he works. He exiled you to this city of all cities? One look at you and I can guess why."

She was finished playing coy? It was about time. I let my gaze sweep over her face, and one side of my mouth curled upward.

In response, she leaned back in her seat, too sure of herself.

"Perhaps he knows you better than you know yourself. Perhaps he is…"

She let her words hang in the air and reached a hand under the table. Her fingers trailed along the inside of my thigh.

"Testing you?" she finished.

I cleared my throat. I'd underestimated her. Her attempt at seduction was laughable, that I expected.

But I hadn't realized she understood the reason I'd been sent. The true reason.

"Maybe you should just give in." She was so close, I felt her breath on my cheek.

I remained silent while I managed my irritation at this woman.

A victorious smile spread across her face. At least, it did until I spoke.

"Did you think he sent me to bed you, Stephanie?" In all honesty, knowing Gavin, I wouldn't put it past him.

She choked on the sip of martini she'd just taken.

I leaned away and checked my watch. "It's late." I rose to my feet.

She cleared her throat, looking around, obviously not expecting things to take this turn.

"I'll get you a taxi." I pulled her chair out.

Unable to do anything else, she stood. I placed a hand at her back to guide her to the coat check. Once there, I helped her with her coat and led her outside. A taxi had just pulled up to the curb.

She turned to me just before entering the vehicle. "You misunderstood," she said, looking embarrassed.

"I'm sure I did. Good night, Stephanie."

I handed the driver some bills to take care of her fare home, then reentered Club Carmen, resuming my seat at the table. I watched Kat play for another hour before, finally, she finished and stood, glancing around the room for the first time.

No one stopped their conversation, no one applauded. But I guessed that wasn't the point. She was background, to set the mood. But how could anyone think of that music as background?

When her gaze fell in my direction, I stopped breathing.

I knew those eyes. She was older, her features sharper, but it was her. Lina. I was sure of it.

With the spotlight on her, she couldn't see me. I studied her from the anonymity of my seat. Last I'd seen her was two years ago. She'd be twenty now. Her hair had grown longer, and she'd dyed it darker than its natural chocolate brown. The contrast between it, her smooth olive skin and mossy-green eyes was striking.

When she turned to leave, I caught sight of the tattoos that disappeared into her dress.

I waved the waitress over and closed out my tab, then walked to the coat check. I didn't even take the time to button up my coat as I walked out and around to the back of the building where I guessed the staff entrance to be. By the time I got there, though, Lina—or Kat—was already halfway down the street, moving quickly through the rain that felt like ice crystals against my face.

I don't know why I didn't call out to her. Instead, I followed her like some stalker, matching her step for step as she walked three blocks then turned left and headed to the subway.

Shit. I needed to buy a ticket. She had a pass, so she swiped and went through.

It took a few minutes to get my ticket. I made my way down, lucky there was only one direction she could go, not thinking about why I was in such a panic to follow her. I took the stairs fast, and by the time I hit the platform, a train arrived, and the doors slid open. I looked right and left, but I didn't see her. A few passengers disembarked, but no one boarded.

Confused, I walked right.

The train doors closed, and I watched it go. Had I missed her?

I stuck around another few minutes, but I was alone on the platform. It was when I turned to leave that I heard it. The sounds of a struggle.

I moved toward the noise. It came from behind a construction blockade.

A man's raspy voice ordered for someone to be quiet. I slowed my steps, but when she screamed, I broke into a run and found two men had cornered her against a blockade. I guessed them to be homeless from the looks of them. One brandished a knife.

I only saw Lina in my periphery, my eyes locked on the men. They were drunk. I could see it and smell it, but they had a weapon, and I had nothing.

"I've called the police. You'd better get out of here before they get here," I warned.

"Fuck you, man."

He looked uncertainly at his partner who held the knife. He jittered from one foot to the other like he was more than just drunk.

I moved closer. "Get behind me," I told Lina, stretching my arm out between the men and her. She obeyed and I stood between them, shielding her from them with my body.

"The bag," the man brandishing the knife said. "Give me the bag."

Footsteps sounded at the top of the stairs.

"Fuck, that's the cops. Let's go!" His friend bolted, leaving the other man to look around, confused and unsure.

"Go!" I yelled.

He ran, obeying the order. I stood with my back to Lina, safeguarding her until I was sure they'd gone.

Lina made a sound behind me, a shaky, audible exhale. I slowly turned.

"That's never happened before."

She was just a few feet from me. I studied her and no matter what the waitress had said her name was, it was Lina. *My* Lina. I had no doubt. "Are you okay? Did they hurt you?"

She sucked in a choppy breath, straightening, her eyes reddening even as she shook her head. "I'm okay."

She looked up at me then, turning striking green

eyes to me. A spark of disbelief flashed through them as she slowly processed who I was.

I stood watching her, too.

"Damon?" she finally asked, breaking the spell.

I ran a hand through my hair. "You're supposed to be in Chicago."

She looked at me, at my black coat. No collar. Not what she expected, I guessed.

"You're supposed to be a priest."

I had no response to that. She was right. I was supposed to have been ordained two years ago. But things had become complicated.

I bent to pick up the things that had fallen out of her bag during her struggle. "You shouldn't be down here alone this late at night."

"I always take this train."

Give me your bag," I said.

She looked confused but handed it over. I put the things back inside.

"Let's go." I gestured to the stairs, keeping her bag in my hand.

"Where?"

"We'll get a taxi."

"What are you doing here? How did you find me?"

"I didn't find you. I just happened to come to Club Carmen. Lina, your sister thinks you're at school in Chicago."

Her eyes widened, and pink flushed her cheeks.

The sound of people singing at the top of the stairs interrupted. More drunks.

"Let's go," I said, growing angry now that the rush of what just happened passed. "You can explain when I get you home."

2

LINA

Once on the street, Damon signaled for a taxi. After opening the door to let me in he slipped in beside me. I just stared at him for a long minute. Seeing him again, god, it was the strangest thing. Like being propelled back in time.

What was he doing here? In Manhattan? I thought, well, I assumed at least, that he'd be ordained by now.

"Lina?"

I shook my head. "Sorry, what did you say?" Had he been talking to me?

"Your address. Where do you live?"

"Oh." Turning to the driver, I rattled off the address to my apartment, then glanced once more at Damon before sitting back in my seat, pretending to look through my purse to organize it. Truth was, I needed to get hold of myself.

"They didn't take anything, did they?"

"No. They would have been disappointed anyway. Not much in here," I said with a weak smile. What was he doing here? No one knew I was in New York City, and I wanted to keep it that way.

The heat was cranked high in the taxi, which smelled like pipe smoke and old food. I pulled my knitted hat off my head and loosened the scarf around my neck before clearing my throat. I turned to him.

"What are you doing here, Damon?"

He watched me, his eyes strange, the blue more somber than I remembered. He'd be about twenty-seven now, but he looked older than I expected.

The last time I'd seen him was a few weeks before I left for Chicago. My sister had given me such a hard time about taking time off between high school and music school that I'd acquiesced. Or at least led her to believe I had.

I hadn't really decided then that I wouldn't attend school. In fact, I had, for the first few months. It just wasn't for me. Not then. There was too much I had to work through and living with Sofia and Raphael in the estate in Tuscany—while it had been wonderful, and I loved them both—I'd needed my own space. I needed time. And I needed to feel all this shit that Sofia, with the best of intentions, had tried to shield me from feeling.

I'd done something terrible, even if, according to the FBI, it was the right thing to do.

I'd betrayed my grandfather. The man who'd taken us in and cared for us. It didn't matter what he'd done. I needed to come to terms with my part in his downfall, and I didn't know how to do that.

But even though I knew I needed to stop and face it, I kept finding myself running at every turn.

"I'm here for half a year," Damon said.

For a moment, I'd forgotten what we were talking about. "Oh." That seemed strange. Why would he be in New York City? I'd always assumed he'd stay in Italy, have a congregation near the Bellini estate. "Why?"

He ignored my question, but I didn't miss the shadow that darkened his eyes.

"The waitress called you Kat."

I looked away as the taxi slowed to a stop. "This is it,'" I said, reaching into my purse for my wallet.

Damon put his hand over mine.

My breath caught in my throat. I looked down at it. At where his big hand covered mine. Then looked at him. It was the most platonic of touches, or at least I was sure it was meant to be, but when I met his gaze, I swear he felt it too, the strange electricity between us.

But that was wishful thinking.

He cleared his throat and pulled his wallet out of his pocket to sort through some bills. After paying the driver, we climbed out of the taxi. I hesitated but knew he wasn't going anywhere. Not yet. Not now.

Damon glanced up and down the pretty, nearly deserted street of beautiful homes. Did he wonder how I afforded to live here?

"This one's mine." I walked up the stairs of the brownstone. Damon followed close behind me. I hadn't forgotten how big he was. How wide his shoulders were. How his presence could be so overwhelming.

It took three tries to slide my key into the lock and turn it before pushing the door open. The flat of Damon's hand came over my head to hold it as we entered. I glanced at it again, like in the taxi, then at him, before climbing the stairs to the second floor where my apartment was. The one I borrowed. Shit. How was I going to explain this? It had to be obvious that this place would be out of my budget.

We stepped into the apartment, and I switched on the light. I slipped off my coat and scarf and hung them on the rack by the door before taking off my hat and setting it and my purse on the table along with my keys.

Damon unbuttoned his coat while I watched, his eyes shifting to my face, an abundance of questions in them. But then his gaze slipped to my shoulder where my sweater had slid over to expose skin.

The tattoos.

They covered the whole of my right arm, shoulder, and most of my back. Flowers in all colors and shapes. All pretty and delicate and pure. I'd designed it myself over many months before finally having the courage to get it done.

I cleared my throat and pulled the sweater up to cover my shoulder before walking into the kitchen.

"Would you like something to drink?" I opened the fridge, pretending to take stock of what I had, although I already knew. "I don't have much. Iced tea or water." I cleared my throat. "Whiskey too," I added, looking at Alexi's bottle of the expensive stuff sitting on the counter. I never touched it, but whenever he dropped by to *'check on his investment,'* as he liked to say, he'd sit on his couch, put his feet up on his coffee table and expect me to pour glass after glass while he watched me.

"Water's fine."

Damon walked over to the window. I watched him take in the not too large but very nicely decorated space with its lush sofa, the dining table with four chairs, the kitchen with its sleek, modern appliances still shiny and new. I never used any of them apart from the coffee machine. I didn't cook. And this wasn't home. It would never be home.

He paused before the large print of an old photo Alexi had blown up to place over the couch when the apartment had become his responsibility several months ago.

I turned my back, not wanting to know what he thought.

Hell, knowing what he *must* think.

"The apartment came furnished. I just live here while the owner's away." Not quite a lie. "It's not mine. None of it is mine."

I snuck a peek in time to see Damon cock his head to the side as he studied the print. It was of two women, one on her hands and knees, her bare ass to the camera. The other woman was crouched on top of her, her blouse open, breasts exposed, an arm raised and about to strike the backside of the woman beneath her.

I felt my face heat up when Damon turned to me. I couldn't meet his gaze when I handed him the bottle of water. "The owner is...eccentric."

"I'd say." He took the bottle. "I have questions, Lina."

"I guess you would."

"Sit," he said.

I didn't question his authority.

Damon remained standing for a long time, then finally perched on the edge of the coffee table.

"You want to tell me what's going on?"

"Not really," I tried with a lopsided grin.

He smiled, his blue eyes brightening.

My belly fluttered. I'd almost forgotten how

disarmingly beautiful he was. He leaned in so his knees touched mine. My mouth went dry as our eyes locked. Did he know how he impacted me? Did he know how hard my heart beat against my chest?

He took the bottle of water I held and twisted the cap off before handing it back to me.

"Relax, Lina."

I blinked several times, glancing at my lap, then back at him. He watched me.

"I'm just...surprised to have run into you here. Surprised by all this." He gestured around him.

I nodded and took a small sip.

"What are you doing here? Why aren't you at school?"

"I..." I cleared my throat. "That school didn't work out for me. It was too...hard." Did my voice rise a little when I lied? Because it was a lie. I'd walked away. It wasn't that I couldn't hack it. Not even close. "I failed the first year. I'd have had to repeat, and I didn't want to do that, so I left. I'm taking some time off. Thinking about what I want to do." When had lying come so easily to me?

"You flunked out?"

He didn't believe me. I heard it in his voice. But I nodded anyway, swallowing hard. "Sofia doesn't know. I didn't want to worry her or stress her out. I want her to be proud of me." Oh wow. Who was this person talking?

"Is that so?"

"Yes."

He stood and turned a circle around the room.

"So you came to New York City. Got some tattoos..." he trailed off.

I gulped another drink of water.

"And are playing piano at Club Carmen, about which I've heard...stories."

"I just play piano. That's all. I don't work the private parties." Guilt made my belly tighten.

"The infamous private parties."

I shouldn't have mentioned that part. Of course, he'd know about them. All of Manhattan knew about them.

"And you're house-sitting?" he continued.

"Sort of." It sounded ridiculous to hear him say it, to hear him tell me the story I'd just made up.

"Sort of?"

"The man who owns the club—owned it—owns the apartment."

Damon looked confused. Well, it was a confusing story. Alexi Markov owned Club Carmen. It had been transferred into his name the day his father, Sergei, had been arrested. Sergei still owned the apartment, even though Alexi liked to act like it was his.

"That would explain the very expensive bottle of whiskey, not to mention the décor." His gaze swept to that damned print again.

"It's temporary." I cleared my throat. "He didn't

want to leave the apartment empty, and I needed a place to stay when I first got here."

"So how long have you had this arrangement?"

Shoot. I hadn't meant to give that away.

"Are you going to tell Sofia?" I asked, ignoring his question.

"What do you think I should do?"

I didn't have to answer, though, because he continued.

"Lina," he paused, a look of disappointment on his face. "What exactly do you have to do for the club owner to be so generous with you?"

I stood. I hated that. Everyone assumed I slept with Alexi, with his dad. It wasn't true, and I was sick of it.

"I'm not sleeping with him if that's what you're implying." I went to him and stood just feet from him. "What right do you have, coming here to question me anyway? This is *my* life."

"I'm glad to see you're so mature about it."

"Fuck you, Damon!" Shit. I just cursed at a priest. Well, an almost priest.

He chuckled. Just chuckled.

"You can't just walk in here and interrogate me."

"I beg to differ. When I find you in New York City when you're supposed to be in Chicago, I don't think it's unreasonable for me to have questions. Questions you will answer."

"Or what?"

His gaze swept down to my mouth and over to my shoulder—damn sweater slipped again. He gave me the smallest of smiles and glanced back at the print.

"Or..." he drew the word out.

I fisted my hands, squeezing the bottle of water I didn't realize I still held until water splashed the sweater at my wrist. "Shoot."

Damon took the bottle and set it down, then closed his hands over my arms, rubbing once, squeezing a little, his smile tight.

"I care about you, Lina. That's why I'm asking."

I blinked a few times, my eyes suddenly misty as I looked up into his. They had darkened since a few minutes ago.

"You were at seminary," I said stupidly. "You're supposed to be a priest."

He lowered his gaze with a resigned exhale, then released my arms and turned his back to look out the window. "This is my final assignment before ordination."

"What do you mean? I thought by now..."

It took him a few minutes to turn back around. Those empty moments felt weighted, heavy.

"Think of me as a slow learner." He tried to make it sound light, but I knew it wasn't. His expression grew serious before he spoke again.

"Maybe like you, I'm trying to figure out who I

am, where I belong." His gaze shot over me. "What I want."

"You don't know?"

He smiled at my question, but it didn't touch his eyes.

"You're not the only one searching, Lina."

I smiled back, feeling like we were on equal footing, at least in this. "Want something to eat?" I asked, walking into the kitchen. "I can scramble a mean egg."

"Sure."

He followed and leaned against the counter while I took the eggs and a pan out. He then opened a couple of cupboards, which I already knew he'd find empty apart from coffee, tea, and a bag of pasta.

"I'm not much of a cook."

"I can see that. You used to like to eat, though."

"I still like to eat. I usually have dinner at the club."

"How many nights do you play?'"

"Four."

"What do you eat the other three nights."

"Oh, you know. I go out or get takeout"

I glanced back to find him eyeing me. I wore an oversize sweater now, but he'd seen me in the slinky black dress at the club. Alexi chose what I wore when I worked. A part of the agreement when he took over the club. I was just glad tonight's dress had been relatively conservative, but he'd still have seen how thin I was.

"You've lost weight since I last saw you."

That was an understatement. I weighed one hundred and five pounds and was 5'5" tall.

I shrugged a shoulder. "I have a high metabolism. Trust me, I eat." God, another lie. But this was to save face. If he knew I had no money, I'd be humiliated. And if he tried to give me some, I think I'd die.

Alexi liked for me to be dependent on him. It was his revenge, I guess. Because he had me now. Not the way he wanted. He hadn't forced that. Not yet, anyway. But he owned me in every other way.

I plated scrambled eggs, grabbed forks, and set the dishes on the counter.

"I have some ketchup," I said as I looked at the plain plate of food. I opened one of the drawers to look for the little packets.

"This is fine."

I sat down, and we ate in silence. Alexi was out of town until tomorrow night, which was a relief. I wouldn't know how to explain Damon to him or how to explain Alexi to Damon if they ever met.

No. I needed to keep Damon as far from Alexi Markov and the Markov family as possible. It was the only way to keep him safe.

"So, you live in New York City?" I asked.

"I've been here about five weeks. I'll be here for at least half a year."

"Can I ask you why?"

He rubbed the back of his neck, his gaze not on me as he considered his answer. "It's complicated."

He didn't want to talk about it. I could understand that, although I was more than a little curious. "How's Sofia?" I asked, my throat tight. I hadn't called my sister in two weeks and felt like a jerk. But truth was, lying to her was getting harder and harder.

"Good. Very pregnant."

"Twins." I smiled. "Is she huge?"

"Getting there. Raphael takes good care of her, though."

"He'd better."

"Why did the waitress call you Kat?" he asked, abruptly changing the subject back to me.

I shrugged a shoulder, wanting to make it appear to be less than it was. "It's my name. Katalina. Lina was what everyone called me from when I was little, so it stuck. I just…I needed to be someone else. Maybe just for a little while. Maybe for longer." I pushed the food around my plate, no longer hungry. "Everyone always decided everything for me, Damon."

I didn't need to look at him to know he was watching me closely. I could feel his gaze on me.

"Do you want me to call you Kat?" he asked.

I turned to him, his question surprising me. "No." There was silence as I stood to clear our plates away. I had my back to him when I next spoke. "I don't want you to tell Sofia."

"You're an adult, Lina. This is your life."

I faced him, smiling, relieved, but then he continued.

"You should tell her yourself. Lying to her, to everyone, that's the part I'm struggling with."

My smile vanished. I felt suddenly angry. A moment ago, I'd felt like maybe he understood. But I was wrong. "Is that leftover priest talk?" I asked, not missing how he winced at my words.

"Lina—"

"Are you going to lecture me? Maybe act like this place is your confessional, and I'm some sinner who's come for absolution? To be forgiven? Or maybe looking for one more person to tell me what I should do with my life? Who I should be?"

"Lina."

He stood but when I tried to scoot past him, he caught me easily.

"What the hell are you talking about?" he asked.

"I don't need you to judge me, and I don't need one more person telling me what's best for me. You don't know anything about me."

"I'm not judging you. And I don't presume to know what's best for you."

"Really? The only person who has to struggle

with anything as far as my life is concerned is me. Not you."

"Where is this coming from?" He appears surprised by the outburst and I get it. So I take a different approach.

"It would worry Sofia if she knew. That's why I didn't tell her. I mean with the pregnancy and—"

"You left school before her pregnancy. You moved to New York City *before* her pregnancy."

I tried to shake him off, but he tightened his grip on my arm and took hold of the other one as well.

"Let me go."

"Why? So you can walk away? Turn your back to me? Is it easier to lie to me then?"

"I'm not... Let go."

"Maybe you hope I'll just go away. Hope I don't ask you questions that obviously make you uncomfortable."

"It's none of your business. None of this is."

"I'm your friend, Lina. Not your enemy."

"Right. My friend."

"And I do have an opinion on the way you've chosen to handle things."

"And you feel free to share those opinions with me, even though I never asked for them. Just like you felt free to look through my kitchen cabinets earlier."

"You are so damn stubborn."

"You don't know me."

"We're not strangers."

"Aren't we?" He seems hurt by that and I feel like a jerk. "Look, I'm just tired of other people thinking they all know what's best for me. As if I can't figure it out for myself."

"Let me ask you a question. What would you have done tonight if I hadn't shown up when I had?"

"That's never happened before." The subway incident had shaken me up too, but it was an isolated event. I'd be more vigilant next time.

"And what if they'd wanted more than your wallet?"

"Jesus, Damon. Nothing happened. Let it go. Let *me* go." I pressed my hands against his chest to push him away, but it was like trying to move a brick wall.

"Nothing happened?" he asked, shaking me once.

"Let me go. Please." My voice cracked. I hated that. I hated weakness.

A moment later, he released me and stepped back. He ran a hand through his hair and shook his head once as if he were shaking off a thought.

"Look, it's late. It's been a long night. Can I see you tomorrow? I'll take you out for dinner. We can start over." He paused and gave me a little smile. "No eggs."

I knew he was trying to make light of it. "I don't—"

"It's dinner. Just dinner. Not an interrogation."

I hesitated. He raised his eyebrows and gave me a smile I remembered. One that always made my belly feel like it was filled with butterflies. He was even better looking than I remembered. His eyes, his mouth, just…him.

This is a bad idea.

"I'd really like a do-over," he added. "For old time's sake."

I studied him for a moment. I wanted a do-over too. "Okay. Dinner's okay."

"Good. I'll pick you up at seven."

"I can just meet you some—"

"I'll pick you up at seven. Good night, Lina," he said and walked out the door.

I stared at the space where he'd just stood for a few moments before going to the window. I saw him appear on the front steps. When he glanced up and saw me, he gave me a little wave, then turned and disappeared into the night.

I watched until he was out of sight, then locked the door and switched off the lights, equally excited and nervous about dinner. Wanting it, wanting to be with Damon, to see him again, and cautious, knowing this couldn't lead anywhere. Knowing I shouldn't get my hopes up. There was too much at stake for that.

3

DAMON

The rain had slowed to a drizzle, so I walked half an hour back to my borrowed apartment at St. Mark's Roman Catholic Church, needing the cool air and the walk to work through what had happened tonight.

Lina Guardia, who should have been studying in a school in Chicago, was living in a very nice apartment in Greenwich Village that her boss owned—free of charge—and working as a pianist in an eclectic club with an illicit reputation.

She was also going by the name Kat, which she explained as being her own name, and although that was true, it fit about as well as her boss letting her live without strings and rent-free in his apartment.

Not to mention the fact that she's been lying to her sister about where she's been for over a year.

The moment I got to my apartment, I took off my

coat and gloves and booted up my laptop. First thing I did was google Club Carmen. That was when things went downhill. I guess I expected them to, because I had a hunch she was lying about school too. She wouldn't have failed. That was too outrageous.

But first, Club Carmen.

Owned by Alexi Markov, son of the infamous Sergei Markov, who currently sat behind bars in a federal prison awaiting trial on charges of racketeering, extortion, money laundering, and murder.

Nice guy.

His son, who from newspaper accounts was as close to his father as any mob family could be, apparently had his sights on taking over the family business once his father was locked up for good.

The apple hadn't fallen far from the tree.

Club Carmen wasn't under investigation. At least when they'd initially looked into it. The feds had found nothing to link it to Sergei's illegal dealings, although it was fishy that it changed hands the day of Sergei's arrest. And not finding something didn't mean there wasn't anything to find.

Question was, how much did Lina know about her employer?

I shut down my laptop and rubbed my face. It was three in the morning. Too late to get anything done.

I considered calling Raphael. It would be nine

o'clock in Italy. But I didn't want to do that just yet. My reasons for that were purely selfish, though. I wanted Lina for myself for a little bit. As wrong as I knew it was, I wanted it, and I wouldn't deny that truth. Wanting it was bad enough. I wouldn't lie to myself about it.

Stripping off my clothes, I took a shower. I needed to figure out how to handle this with her. If I didn't do this right, if she thought for one moment I was attacking her, she'd shut down. Shut me out. I couldn't afford that.

And I had a feeling she couldn't either.

I RANG Lina's doorbell at a little after seven the next evening. Instead of buzzing me up, she quickly appeared, her coat half on as she walked out of the building, giving me a glimpse of the ripped jeans and tight-fitting white shirt with gold block lettering across her chest. She stopped to button her coat then turned her face up to mine, smiling.

"Where to?"

She looked beautiful, her hair hanging in long waves, her face dewy, glossy lips fuller than I remembered them. I cleared my throat. "I heard about this Middle Eastern place," I said, leading her toward the waiting taxi. "It's not too far and is supposed to be pretty good."

"I love Middle Eastern."

Her high heels clicked as she descended the steps and climbed into the taxi, her mood much lighter than it had been last night, even if she did seem in a hurry to get away from her apartment.

I followed her into the taxi and gave the driver the address. Lina punched something into her phone then dropped it into her purse and turned to me.

"What do you do when you're not working?" I asked.

"I have a couple of kids I teach piano to. Little kids, I mean. I think their parents just enjoy having me around to babysit really, but I don't mind. It's fun, and the kids are nice. Other than that," she shrugged a shoulder, "not much, I guess." She hesitated. "Friends of mine have a band, and I sometimes play with them. You know, if it works out."

"A band?"

She nodded, seeming almost embarrassed. "Just some friends I met at a bar."

I could guess how she got into bars at twenty but didn't pursue it.

We reached the restaurant. I paid the driver, got out, and helped Lina exit the cab. It was hard to not think of this as a date, especially when, as we walked into the noisy café and she took off her coat every eye in the place turned to her.

I wasn't surprised. Lina was beautiful but dressed

like she was in knee-length, high-heeled black boots, a pair of ripped jeans that hugged her ass and thighs, and a shirt with only one sleeve that left her tattooed shoulder and arm exposed, she was something to see.

After handing our coats to the girl behind the coat check, I set one hand at her lower back, fingers curling around her waist, knowing how possessive my action would feel, would appear, but not caring. I couldn't stand the thought of others looking at her. And they *were* looking as we followed the hostess to a booth at the far back, close to the band sitting on cushions and playing Middle-Eastern music on a low stage.

If Lina thought how I held her was strange, she didn't say so. She only gave me a hooded glance but didn't pull away. In fact, she seemed to stand closer. Maybe liking it. Because on some level, as wrong as it was, I liked it too.

We sat down, and when the waitress came, ordered drinks—a Coke for her and a beer for me—as well as some appetizers. She turned to me.

"This is great. I love the music."

I smiled, so many thoughts circling inside my head. "It's really good to see you again, Lina."

"You too, Damon."

Silence descended between us until the waitress returned with our drinks and appetizers. Lina picked up a piece of pita bread, dipped it into the hummus, and bit off a chunk.

"I'm starving."

I watched her choose a second triangle of bread and followed her lead.

She read the menu as she absently picked up one of the meatball appetizers and popped it into her mouth. All I could do was look at her, study her every move, memorize her every feature as if her being absent for the last two years had meant more than it had. More than it could.

I cleared my throat. "Do you know what you'd like for dinner?"

"I think the kebabs. Or the falafel. I can't decide. You?" she asked, turning to me.

The waitress came by before I could answer, and I glanced at Lina. "She'll have the kebabs and a side order of falafel, and I'll have the lamb chops."

Once the waitress left, Lina picked up her Coke and turned to me. "I'm going to look like a pig when my plate comes."

I shrugged a shoulder. "You can stand to eat."

She picked up another meatball. "So you live here now? Where exactly?"

"About half an hour's walk from your place at one of the two apartments at St. Mark's Church. One is used by the parish priest, Father Leonard, and the other has been empty for a few months, so I'm using it while I'm here."

"Do you…" her forehead wrinkled. "Say mass?"

"I can't say Mass, but I can give sermons and just help out a little."

"What happens when the six months are up? Are you a priest then? Ordained?"

"It depends. I could be." How did I explain what I was feeling? What I was thinking?

"If you don't want to talk about it, it's fine."

"It's not that I don't want to talk about it. I just haven't. I guess I'm doing a little bit of what I accused you of last night." I knew I'd have to gain her trust to get her to talk to me, to tell me what was going on, and if that meant I went first, then I'd do that. "I guess the best way to say this is that this is my last opportunity to say no. To decide I don't want this."

"Is that why you're here? In New York City?"

"Partially, I guess. I'm also working to secure funding for the seminary."

"Are you having doubts?"

I couldn't answer that. I didn't want to, because I didn't want to say it out loud.

"Things changed after Raphael came home. In a way, back when I first entered seminary, it was a safe place. But I realized soon enough it was a way for me to run away from everything, from all the crap that happened to my family." Her shoulders slumped, and she glanced away for a moment, but I went on. "I don't know how much you know about

Raphael or our father or what he did to us. To him."

"Just tell me everything."

"From a very young age, I remember feeling like our father had a special hatred for him especially. Not for me. Not for Zach. Just Raphael. I didn't understand it, because we were twins. Identical, at least physically. Although Raphael grew faster than me. Throughout our teenage years, he was a little bigger. But maybe that was because he was always fighting too. At school or with cousins or friends. It was almost like his anger made him harder. I always wonder if that anger was what made our father hate him, turn on him like he did, or if his hatred of Raphael made Raphael so angry. So hard."

"The chicken and the egg."

It took me a minute to continue. I'd never said this out loud.

"Our father beat Raphael. He didn't touch Zach or me, but he'd whip Raphael—often until he bled. Sometimes longer than that. I watched it happen a few times. When our father threatened me, Raphael would step in. I always wondered if father did that on purpose. If he knew that, no matter what, Raphael would take the beating."

"I knew he was abusive, but I didn't know that. He was sick."

"My mother was a devout Catholic. Forgiveness is divine—or it was to her. Maybe I wanted it to be for me too. I try to think that everyone has dark and light inside them, good and evil, but my father?" I shook my head. "His soul was as black as Satan's."

After clearing our appetizers, the waitress returned with our meals, giving me a few minutes to think. I had never talked about this. Most people didn't ask.

"After the fire, when Raphael went to prison, I became guardian of our younger brother, Zach, who was sixteen at the time. The house went to Raphael, since he was firstborn—"

"You're twins."

"He has a few minutes on me." I winked, watched her smile. "Zach and I lived in it with Maria, who'd been our cook and nanny ever since I could remember. The memories in that place, Lina, they haunted me. My parents were dead. My brother was in prison. And the past clung to the very walls in that house. After a while, I couldn't breathe. The one thing that gave me solace was the chapel. I'd go there often, just sit in a pew and listen to the silence, try to make sense of everything. I guess that's when I decided I should become a priest. It was a selfish decision made purely with myself in mind. I didn't care about helping anyone else. I just wanted to... No, I needed to get out of my head. The church made me feel closer to my mother, and in a way, that was sanity. It gave me direction and routine and gave me something to think about that wasn't me or my past or what happened to the Amado family."

"So you were running away."

"Yes."

"And the dean sent you here to figure out if the priesthood is what you really want?"

"Yes and the moment I feel like I've made up my mind, something comes along to make me question."

Or someone.

She bit into a piece of falafel, studying me. "I thought it was a waste anyway," she said, then turned her attention to her plate.

"What do you mean?"

"Damon, look at you. Every woman in this place —and some of the men too—turned to look when we walked to our table."

"Sweetheart, it was you they were looking it. Not me." I gave her a wink.

She blushed and glanced away for a moment.

"Besides, that doesn't matter."

When she returned her gaze to mine, her eyes had grown serious.

"So you have six months to figure out your life?"

"It looks that way."

"What do you want?"

"My six months aren't up yet," I said, taking my last sip of beer, glad I'd already put my glass down when she next spoke, abruptly changing the subject.

"I was the one who turned over the evidence that put my grandfather away."

I studied her as she focused on her plate, pushing her food around. I guess we were being honest. "I know."

"There's one thing I didn't tell Sofia, though. One thing I didn't tell anyone." She finally looked up at me. "They thought I told them everything."

She paused, then gave a nervous giggle. Her face darkened almost in the same instant.

"I probably could go to jail for it."

"What's the one thing?" I asked, everything growing much more serious suddenly.

Her eyes grew wet and the tip of her nose reddened. She shook her head. "I'm going to explode if I eat one more bite, Damon."

I looked at her plate, which was nearly empty. "You made an impressive dent. Would you like dessert?"

She shook her head. "Let's get out of here. I want to show you something. If you want to, I mean. That band I told you about is playing tonight. Would you like to see them? They're really great, and the location is...well, you'll appreciate it."

"Sounds great."

I signaled for the waitress to bring the check, and once I'd paid, we got our coats. I helped Lina into hers, studying the details of her exposed tattoos without being observed by her at least for a moment. I wanted hours to do it, though.

Once outside, I went to hail a taxi, but she stopped me with a hand on my arm.

"Let's walk. It's only about twenty minutes, and it's not raining or snowing for a change."

"Okay. Lead the way."

I tucked her arm into mine. She seemed surprised at first but gave herself over to it and we walked, the night air cold against our faces. We didn't speak and, about twenty minutes later, we came upon an old church tucked between two large buildings.

She slipped her arm from mine. I looked at the building, then at her.

"It's called Redemption," she said. "Obviously, it was a church once. Is that going to be weird for you?"

I smiled. "No. Not weird. I'm intrigued."

I opened one of the large double doors where a bouncer sat just inside. I wondered how she was going to get in since she was underage, but she smiled at the man, who called her by name and looked me over from head to toe as she hugged him.

"Kat, it's good to see you," he said, turning his attention to her.

"It's good to see you, R.J. This is my...brother-in-law, Damon."

"Brother-in-law, huh?"

"Yes. My sister is married to his brother."

R.J. took a minute, then extended his hand. "Good to meet you, man."

"Good to meet you."

"Go on in. It's busy tonight."

"Thanks," she said, taking my hand again to lead me inside.

The church was small but pretty, each of the four corners arched. The stained-glass windows were still in place, and incense scented the air. I always liked the smell.

Two long bars stood at opposite ends, and a stage had been erected against the far wall. Music played, and people danced or stood around in groups talking and drinking. Wooden stools were the only seats in the place, which was as opposite to Club Carmen in feel, sound, and sight, as you could possibly get.

"Want a drink?" she asked as we reached the bar. She was still tentative. Maybe she realized the ice she walked on was thin. She'd need to come clean with me at some point.

The bartender wiped his hands on a towel and approached her with a smile.

"Kat. It's been a few weeks."

"I've been working, Shawn," she said, making a face.

"I keep telling you that you should quit that uptight place and come work for me."

She smiled and turned to introduce me. "This is my friend, Damon. Damon, this is Shawn."

The bartender nodded coolly. "Usual for you, Kat?"

"Please."

"What'll you have?" he asked me.

I ordered one of the beers on tap.

A few moments later, we had our drinks. Lina snagged a stool, leaned her back against the bar, and watched the empty stage as she sipped from a straw.

"What are you drinking?" I asked when she caught me staring at her.

"Just a Coke." She rolled her eyes. "Don't worry, Shawn won't serve me alcohol until I'm twenty-one."

"I wasn't worried, just curious. Running into you in the city, this whole thing, it's just not what I would ever have expected from you."

"What does that mean?"

"I'm glad it happened, that's all."

"When are you going to spring your questions on me?"

"I'm not." That seemed to surprise her.

"Why not?"

"You'll tell me when you're ready."

"What if I'm not ever ready?"

"I have my ways."

She blushed, focused on drinking her coke. "This is a change from last night," she said without quite looking at me.

"I was unprepared for last night."

"Yeah. Me too."

"You look good, Lina. The tattoos, I like them. It's you, if that makes sense."

She looks at me sideways like she's trying to make out if I'm lying or making fun of her. "Thanks." She blushes again. "It's maybe the only thing that's me right now," she paused. "What do you think my sister will think when she sees?"

"Are you worried about that?"

She considered her half-full glass. "I try not to think about it, honestly. I know it's stupid. I mean, I can't hide out forever."

"Why do you feel like you have to hide out at all? You're an adult, and she's a reasonable person. Just tell her the truth."

"It's complicated, Damon."

I watched her as she spoke, saw how her eyes reddened again, growing moist with tears.

"I do have one question I'd like you to answer."

"You said—"

"Just one."

"Okay," she said, although with hesitance.

"Are you in trouble, Lina?"

Her eyes grew wide, almost panicked. Like a deer in headlights.

And I had my answer.

But before either of us could speak, a group of three came toward her calling out her name, the girl with the pink hair falling into Lina as she hugged her. I stood back and watched, saw how the men smiled but hung back. Shawn handed the girl a drink and gave her a wink.

"It's so good to see you, Jana. I love the pink." Lina touched the girl's long hot-pink hair. "This is Damon."

No *my brother-in-law* or *my friend*. Just Damon.

"Damon, this is Jana, my absolute best friend. She's the singer of the band I was telling you about. She and Shawn are engaged to be married. And these two are Jace and Benji."

"Nice to meet you." I shook hands with them.

"It's about time Kat brought someone with her."

Jana said then returned her attention to Lina and took her hands.

"You're playing a couple of songs with us, right?"

Lina's smile widened, and her eyes sparkled. "I thought you'd never ask."

"Come on," Jana pulled Lina off her stool.

Lina tuned to me. "Do you mind?"

"Are you kidding? I'd love to hear you play."

A moment later, I took the stool Lina had vacated and ordered another beer as the band walked up onto the stage.

I would probably describe the music as punk with the piano accompaniment adding a touch of something darker, something almost gothic, different than the classical she'd played at Club Carmen.

I watched her, studied her face, saw her severe concentration, her intensity. She played with a passion that carried into her music, displaying her pain for anyone who cared to notice.

That was what I'd heard the first time I'd come into Club Carmen. Heartbreak. The music she made sounded like a heartbreak. And for reasons I couldn't explain, I wanted to hear her make a different kind of music. I wanted to take that heartbreak away.

"She's very talented," Shawn, the bartender, said.

I turned to find him studying me before returning his attention to wiping down the counter.

"She is that."

"Special kid."

I felt like he was making some point. I faced him squarely. "I've known Li...Kat since she was sixteen. I know how special she is. I'm glad to see she has friends here looking out for her."

What did I want to say? That I wasn't one of the wolves in sheep's clothing that he need look out for? Because ever since last night, I hadn't been able to get her out of my mind.

And I'd be a liar if I said my thoughts were wholly pure.

Hell, maybe he was right to question me.

The music changed then, and the lights on stage

focused on Lina. The rest of the band took a background role as she began to play something more recent by a popular band only this version was a thousand times more intense as she pounded the keys, her focus unbreakable.

When she finished, there was one single moment of silence before the crowd broke into cheers.

Lina gave a faint smile and turned to me. When she did, I saw how her eyes glistened, how they looked at me with an unfathomable emotion. Something full of longing.

And it slammed me like a fist to the gut.

Jana came around the piano, breaking our locked gaze to hug Lina. I set my glass on the bar and caught the bartender watching me. Scrutinizing me, maybe. He hadn't missed the exchange between Lina and me.

The band took a break. Lina came toward me as dance music pulsed around the bar. She took the Coke the bartender set in front of her, complimenting her. She blushed, obviously uncomfortable with the attention. I watched her, took in her flushed face, the little bit of sweat that dampened her forehead. She set her glass down and took my arm.

"Dance with me."

She began to pull me toward the crowd of dancers jumping and pulsing en masse. I shook my head. "You go ahead," I said, not wanting to dance but wanting to watch her dance. Wanting nothing else in that moment.

She tugged again, her gaze falling on Jana, who waved her over from the dance floor.

"Go," I urged.

"Sure?"

I nodded. She went. I watched her on the dance floor, her body as if it were made for dancing. Hips swaying, her every move sensual, erotic even.

Her hair whipped around her, and although she danced with Jana, men circled her like wolves. As I watched, my hand tightened around my drink and my gaze grew hard.

It took all I had not to drag her away from within the circle of men that formed around them, and the moment I realized she was aware of it, of her power, it took me back.

She turned away from Jana to dance with one man, then another, but all the while she did, she watched me. Her gaze never left mine.

When one of the jerks wrapped his hands around her hips and drew her close, I set my drink down on the bar, beer splashing my fingers. I walked over to them, not caring that I stood like a brick wall on the dance floor, my gaze burning into hers.

I gripped the guy's arm.

They stopped dancing, both of them turning to me.

"Leave," I said to him without ever looking at him.

"What? No, man, we're dancing."

I turned to him, stepped even closer to him. "I said leave." I wasn't sure what had come over me but even my voice sounded different. Animal.

He opened his mouth, closed it again and gave Lina one glance before doing as I told him.

With one hand at her belly, I walked her backward off the dance floor and to a corner. I looked at her. Even with heels the top of her head barely hit my chin and she had to crane her neck to look up at me, all big green eyes, glossy lips. Pretty pink tongue.

Fuck.

I put my forearms on either side of her head and I could see how the pulse beat at her neck. How her pupils dilated.

What the fuck was I doing?

"You like it," I said.

"Like what?"

"This game."

"Game?"

"You like them looking at you. You like *me* looking at you."

She stood up taller and I leaned in closer, close enough to smell her shampoo.

"What do you want, Damon? What do you want right now? If nothing else mattered, what would you want right this second?"

My gaze fell to those lips again and I picked up another scent. Something musky.

It was the smell of want. Of sex.

She wanted to know what I wanted? She knew it already. I could see it in her eyes, feel it as she pressed her hardened nipples against my chest.

And I had no doubt she felt the steel bar my dick had become at her belly.

I knew perfectly well what I wanted.

But there was one difference between us.

I knew what was allowed.

And I knew better what was forbidden.

She put her hands on my chest, tentative at first, then flat against the muscle, feeling it, and fuck me, I should have pushed away, walked away. Dragged her out of here with all these men around her. These men ogling her.

But I didn't.

I leaned down to whisper to her and even for the loud music it was like we were the only two in the place. "You want to know what I want?" My voice came out low and hoarse. More like a warning than anything else.

She licked her lips, anticipating.

Our eyes locked, a charge between us as every breath she took had her nipples scratching against my chest. What I'd give to take one into my mouth. What I'd give to put my mouth somewhere else.

"I want something I can't ever have," I said because fuck me. What the fuck was I doing?

Abruptly, I took her by the arm and spun her toward the exit.

"What are you doing?"

Her smile faded, something akin to fear momentarily passing across her eyes.

"Taking you home, little girl."

She resisted but I didn't care. It's not that I was angry with her. No. I was angry with myself.

"You're hurting me," she finally said when we got outside. It had started raining by now.

I turned to her, saw how tightly I held onto her. Taking a deep breath in, I forced myself to exhale and relaxed my grip a little. Raising my other hand, I hailed a passing taxi who pulled up to the curb.

"I'll walk," she said when I opened the door.

"Get in."

"I said I'll walk."

"I said you'll get in."

"I'm not a little girl, Damon!"

I looked her over. "You think I don't see that?" I shook my head. "Fuck. Get in the cab. Get in before I do something stupid."

She blinked, looking like she wanted to say something but deciding not to. She got into the taxi and I climbed in after her. I gave the driver her address.

We didn't talk for the entire ride. And when we

got back to her place, she climbed out, her attention on digging her keys out of her purse.

"Thanks for dinner," she said as she started climbing up the stairs of the brownstone.

I paid the driver and followed her up. She tried to slip inside when she got the door opened but I followed her.

"I'm fine. You can go," she said, refusing to look at me as she fumbled to unlock that door.

I closed my hand over hers, taking the key and unlocking it myself. I opened the door and held out the key.

She stepped into her apartment and looked down at my open palm like she expected me to snatch her hand when she took it. I didn't.

"Good night," she said, barely able to look at me. I stood in the door so she couldn't close it.

"You never answered my one question."

Her gaze searched mine, and I knew she remembered it. The one when I'd asked her if she was in trouble.

"Can't you leave it alone? Leave me alone?"

"No. On both counts."

She sighed deeply.

And I felt like a dick already for what I'd done in that club, cornering her like that. Wanting her like that. What the fuck is wrong with me? I've known her since she was a girl.

"Give me your phone, Lina."

"Why?"

"Give it to me."

She searched inside her bag for it and after unlocking it handed it over.

I programmed my number into it and hit send.

My phone rang and I saved her number then handed the phone back.

"I'm going to give you tonight. But tomorrow morning, I expect a call with a time and place to meet. I know where you live, and I know where you work. You can't hide from this or from me."

"That doesn't sound too stalker-ish."

If she was trying to go for light, she failed.

"I'm not letting this go. Don't make me come get you. If you do, there will be consequences."

Her eyes grew wide at the warning.

"Understand?"

When she didn't answer, I stepped closer and took her chin in my hand, tilting her face upward. "I asked you a question." There was the fast-beating pulse again, that licking of those too-full lips.

"You said you'd wait for me to tell you when I was ready."

"I must have forgotten to mention the time limit on that. You're going to call me in the morning. Am I clear?"

She nodded.

"Good girl."

4

DAMON

I jerked off to thoughts of Lina.

I should be ashamed to admit it. Hell, maybe I should be in the confessional now. Any honorable man—no, not man. Priest. Any honorable priest would be. I am not very honorable these days, though. Because the thought of her pressed up against the wall like that, the smell of her, the feel of her hard little nipples against me, well, fuck, it makes my dick hard all over again.

I guess it's a good thing I've got the cassock to hide my erection.

Fuck.

As I have done every morning since arriving at St. Mark's, I went into the small chapel to prepare things for Father Leonard's ten o'clock mass. Apart from me, there would be only one attendee, an eighty-year-old widow who attended mass daily. I had a feeling it was her only outing.

If Father Leonard noticed anything unusual about me, he didn't mention it. But I had to admit that throughout the mass, I was distracted.

Once back at my apartment I dialed the number of the small school Lina should have been attending in Chicago. One of the teachers I knew from seminary now taught there, and although it was a violation of Lina's privacy, I decided finding out the details of her departure were necessary for her own good.

The fact that one of her complaints was that everyone was doing everything *for her own good* wasn't lost on me, but this was too important.

Father Aaron, her counselor at the school, hesitated at first, but I explained the situation honestly, although not wholly. He remembered Lina well, liked her from what I gathered. And he sounded disappointed about how she'd left the school.

She'd had great promise, which I knew, but she never quite fit in, never tried to make friends, and kept to herself for the few months she was in attendance.

Months.

Not a full year.

Her grades had been fine, excellent in fact. She'd have made the Dean's list if she'd kept on the track she was on. But out of the blue, she'd met with him to tell him she was leaving. That she needed time. Told him exactly what she'd told me last night.

Except that she hadn't told her sister or Raphael that she up and left.

She'd lied to me, and she'd lied well. Casually, almost.

I gave Lina until noon to call me but she didn't. I wasn't surprised.

Did she wonder about the consequences I mentioned? Did she think I was kidding?

After dinner, I showered and changed into dark slacks and a black button-down shirt, put on my coat and gloves, and headed out. I caught a taxi and got to Club Carmen about twenty minutes later.

I arrived at prime time, and when I walked inside, I felt a sense of relief when I heard the piano music. It was her. I didn't have to see her to know. But tonight's music sounded darker, more intense.

I made my way to the bar in the main room where the piano was located. Lina wore a red dress tonight, the fit tight, the color a striking contrast with her hair and skin. It had spaghetti straps and a plunging back. I caught sight of the tattoos again and swallowed hard when I realized they covered almost the whole of her back, disappearing into her dress. Flowers. So many flowers, color upon color, as if she were a bouquet.

Not for you.

I banished that voice to the farthest recesses of my mind.

My cock twitched at the sight of all that skin. At the memory of her dancing last night. Of her breasts, nipples tight, pressing against my chest. Her pulse beating a staccato.

Thing was, since the day I'd first laid eyes on her four years ago, I'd been drawn to her. She'd been sixteen, though. Off-limits. And I'd been studying to become a priest.

I'd had doubts before I'd met Lina. The thought that I'd used the church to run from my problems—that I was running from facing the past—was always there. But after Lina, after that day we'd spent together—it wasn't just in the background anymore. It took center stage.

"Something to drink?"

The bartender's question jarred me from my thoughts.

"Whiskey neat."

He nodded, and a moment later, I had a tumbler in my hand. I sat and watched her.

She looked up several times over the next two hours, seeming more distracted than she had been when I'd been here last. I made sure she couldn't see me.

At midnight, her shift ended. She rose to her feet and seemed to be in a hurry as she gathered her things. The dress, like a second skin, softly draped as it hugged her body, and fell asymmetrically to just below her knees. Thin leather straps bound red high-heeled sandals to her feet. She wore no bra. I could see that even from this distance. And some part of me, it didn't like it. Didn't like that others could look at her. See her.

When she turned her back to the room, my gaze roamed the length of her, my breathing coming tighter, my cock, once again, reacting. I finished the last of my second whiskey and moved to rise when, from behind the door she'd use to exit the room, emerged a man about my age, shorter than me, wearing a tuxedo. I instantly wanted to wipe the grin he wore off his face.

"Who's that?" I asked the bartender, although after my research I could guess.

"Alexi Markov. Owns the club. His father owns the building."

Lina stopped short at seeing him. I could tell from this distance that she was surprised by his sudden appearance. He stood too close to her. She held a small clutch in one hand. I saw her free hand fist as he extended his to take hers.

Riveted to the spot, I watched their brief interaction, and it spoke volumes.

He said something. She gave him a half smile, then dropped her gaze to her feet. When she wouldn't open her hand to him, he took her small wrist, bent it, and twisted her arm slightly, forcing her to look up at him. Again, he spoke. This time, though, she didn't pretend to smile.

She was afraid of him.

I could see it from here.

Hell, I could feel it.

And I bet he could too.

I took a step toward them, but what happened next surprised me. She pulled her arm free, said two words, and disappeared behind the door he'd come from. He turned to follow her, but someone interrupted. A woman. He replaced the sneer on his face with a wide, toothy smile and turned to his new guest.

I quickly paid and moved through the club to retrieve my coat. Like the other night, I went around the block to the exit she'd use. Unlike that night, though, I actually caught her leaving, her coat half on, her high heels clicking as she rushed out.

She stopped dead when she saw me, and I swear I saw tears in her eyes. But they were quickly gone as she shook her head once and drew her coat closed. She still wore the dress. The other night, she'd changed into jeans and an oversize sweater. Tonight, she'd freeze with just the sleeveless, backless dress beneath her coat, not to mention the sandals more fitting a tropical location.

I turned to hail a taxi, and when it came, I opened the back door for her.

Without a word, she climbed into the cab. I

followed her in and gave the driver her address. But Lina shook her head.

"No. Somewhere else. Anywhere."

I studied her face. She wouldn't quite look at me but fixed her gaze forward.

"All right." Without hesitating, I told the driver to take us to my apartment. What the hell I was doing, I didn't know. All I knew was I needed to be with her. To be alone with her.

We didn't speak on the ride. Didn't say a word as I paid and led her around the side of the church to the entrance of my apartment, grateful the door of the one Father Leonard occupied was on the other side of the building. She didn't hesitate to go where I led her with the slightest touch of my fingers on her lower back. I had a feeling she, like me, wanted to be out of sight as quickly as possible.

I unlocked the outer door, and we ascended the stairs to the second floor, where my studio apartment was over the church. Once we stepped inside, I turned to her as she stopped to take in the small space—a living-room, dining-room combination with a small kitchen. My bed at the opposite corner. Her apartment was about twice as big.

While she studied the surroundings, I studied her. Her long, dark hair was piled high on her head tonight, her lips colored a deep, dark red, lashes thick with mascara and liner.

As beautiful as she looked, I wanted it off. This wasn't Lina.

"Go into the bathroom and wash your face," I told her, closing the door behind us.

Lina faced me, confused. "What?"

"Take it off." I pointed to the bathroom, unsure why I felt so angry, so fucking possessive. But it's like when it came to her, I lost all control.

She looked like she wanted to say something, maybe ask me what the fuck was wrong with me, but instead, she obeyed. Sliding off her coat, she handed it to me, then went into the bathroom and closed the door behind her. I watched that closed door, standing like an idiot holding her coat, still wearing mine, listening to the water run.

Shaking myself out of it, I set her coat over the back of a chair and put mine on top.

I went into the kitchen and grabbed the bottle of whiskey and two glasses before returning to the living area. I poured us each a drink and took my glass to the window, where I gazed out onto the street at the few people strolling outside, not seeing anything at all. I swallowed the contents of my glass and set it down on the side table.

Absently, I rolled up my shirt sleeves before pouring myself a second drink and sitting on the couch to wait for her, knowing exactly what I wanted to do.

Knowing how wrong it would be.

Lina emerged a few minutes later, her hair out of its bun and in one long braid over her shoulder. She stood there, not moving, letting me take her in, in her dress and four-inch heels, only that fine silk standing between us, keeping me from seeing.

And I wanted to see.

I wanted more badly than anything to see.

"I poured you a drink." My voice sounded foreign to my ears.

She looked to where I gestured, opened her mouth, but closed it again. She crossed the room while I watched her and picked up the glass, then forced it down all at once, squeezing her eyes shut as it burned her throat.

I watched her. Couldn't take my eyes off her. And I liked that the whiskey burned. I wanted to punish her.

"You lied to me," I said.

She blinked, having the grace to look away momentarily, not denying what I said. We remained silent, studying each other.

"Take off your dress, Lina." I took a sip of my whiskey and leaned back, crossing one leg over the other.

"My dress?"

"Take it off."

I saw her nipples pebble beneath the silk as her throat worked to swallow. The air in the room suddenly seemed charged with electricity, alive and sparking and ready to electrocute us both.

Lina moved slowly, reaching her hands to either strap and, with her eyes locked on mine, she pulled the dress down to her waist and paused there, letting me look at her, at her small, high breasts with their dark, pebbled nipples.

I swallowed another sip of my whiskey and nodded for her to go on ignoring the voice that was asking me what the fuck I thought I was doing.

Hooking her thumbs into either side of the dress, she pushed it over her hips and let it fall to the floor. She stepped out of it, shoving it aside as if it were a scrap of nothing. She stood with her arms at her sides wearing black lace panties, thigh-high stockings, and high heels.

I let my gaze travel over her, hovering at the slit of her shaved sex visible beneath the lace. I then dragged it back up over her flat belly, pelvic bones jutting out—too skinny—and up over breasts I wanted to take whole into my mouth and suck on until she called out my name. Until she begged me for more.

I forced my gaze to hers.

"Do you do this for him?" I had to ask. I had no choice.

Wide green eyes stared back at me. She knew exactly what I meant. Who I meant.

She didn't open her mouth to speak. Didn't try to explain anything. But she shook her head once.

No.

And I couldn't put words to the relief I felt at that knowledge.

My cock pressed hard against my trousers. I uncrossed my legs and set my glass aside.

"Come here."

She obeyed, moving slowly.

I leaned forward, and once she was close enough, I took her hands and drew her to stand between my knees. Close up, I could smell her sex. Her arousal. A musky, light scent. I kept hold of her tattooed arm and traced the flowers with the fingers of my other hand.

I wanted to punish her. To hurt her for lying to me. To hurt her for that man having touched her. For wearing that dress. For showing herself to them, to all those men and women in that club who watched her with lust in their eyes. Who wanted her.

I wanted to hurt her for all of it.

The hairs on her arms stood on end, and her breathing came short, choppy. She had to feel what I was feeling. Had to know what was coming.

Keeping hold of her wrist, I drew her to the side and pulled her down across my lap. With one hand on the base of her skull, I pushed her face into the seat of the couch and looked at her there, over my lap, naked, or almost so. I studied her tattoo for a long time. She didn't move.

Her back tightened with my first touch, but then she relaxed again.

I took my time caressing every inch of her, every tiny bud inked into her skin, finding a small bird—a robin—I hadn't noticed before. I was suddenly, irrationally jealous of the man or woman who'd held the needle to mark her, jealous of anyone else who had ever touched her. Who had ever looked at her or at these flowers. All these fucking flowers.

My cock throbbed. I needed release. I could jerk off right now, come all over her, mark her as mine. I could come just looking at her like this.

I adjusted my legs, shifting my gaze to her ass now lifted higher than the rest of her. Did she know what I intended? Taking hold of the top of her lace panties, I dragged them down to bare her ass.

Lina shifted slightly, made a small sound, but remained bent over my lap. She didn't move to cover herself.

I took her in, her pale, pristine ass, the shadow of her sex between her cheeks, the scent of her.

I knew that if I touched her now, she'd be wet.

She'd be dripping.

I knew it. I could see it.

Hell, I could smell it.

But I couldn't think about that. Not yet. Not if I didn't want to blow right in my pants.

My fingers caressed her thigh, slowly rising to her hip, circling her ass.

"You are so fucking beautiful." My voice came out hoarse, like it had caught in my throat. "And so fucking bad for me."

She shifted, and when I glanced at her, I found her resting her cheek on the couch, watching me. She arched her back then, offering herself to me. Offering her ass for punishment.

"Don't look at me," I said. I had to. I couldn't have her see me. Not now. Not right now.

She turned her face away but kept her body prone, her ass tilted upward. Anxiety rolled off her, but also something else. Desire. Want. Need.

We both wanted this.

Maybe we both needed it.

Gripping her waist to keep her steady, I raised my hand, all the while warnings sounded in my head, warnings I would not heed. It was out of my control. Tonight, this, me, Lina…it was all out of my fucking control.

I struck.

She gasped, and the sound bounced off the walls. After a full minute, I slapped her other cheek, her skin already turning pink, my handprint clear.

I held her to me as she struggled. And she did struggle, but it was halfhearted. She wanted to be here like this. Over my lap. She needed to be.

She didn't ask me to stop. Instead, she buried her

face into the sofa cushion to muffle her cries. She didn't reach back to cover herself but gave me her wrists to hold at her lower back as I kept her close to me.

I struck ten times. Only ten. One cheek, then the other, measuring each stroke, timing every one while watching the pale flesh redden.

When it was finished, my breathing was raspy, and my cock throbbing for release. I lay my hand over her punished ass. It felt hot to the touch.

Neither of us moved. I rubbed away the sting, almost unable to breathe, to think, that voice accusing me of sin weaker for my arousal, easily shoved aside. I'd have to deal with that, but not now. Later.

Because right now, all I had, all I needed, was this moment. Her. Here. Like this.

Lina shifted. I turned to find her watching me again, her eyes soft, bright, pupils dilated, lips parted and swollen as if she'd been biting them.

I didn't stop her when she slid off my lap to kneel between my legs. I just watched her there, naked and watching me, hands on my thighs, eyes wide. I touched my thumb to her forehead, as if in blessing —even though I knew I had no right—then cupped the back of her head, caressing her soft hair, and for a moment, I remembered what had mattered so much to me once. What had fallen away the day I'd seen her.

Christ.

I'd known it then.

She lay her cheek on my lap, and I petted her. I just petted her.

When she moved her hand to rest it over my erection, I swallowed.

I should have stopped her. I knew I should.

But I didn't.

I couldn't.

Slowly and never looking away, she undid my belt and unzipped my pants. I shifted a little when she cupped my cock and balls, freeing them. She knelt up.

Again, I didn't stop her. I didn't push her away. Not when she wet her lips. Not when she touched her little pink tongue to the tip of my cock and licked away the precum.

No.

Instead, I closed my eyes and twined my fingers into her hair and drew her closer, letting her take me into her mouth, her wet, hot mouth.

"Fuck." I let out a moan as she took me deeper, softly at first, moving slowly, licking my length and sucking, and when I opened my eyes and our gazes met, I tightened my hold on her hair and drew her closer, guiding her to swallow my dick, pressure building as I thickened.

"Fuck, Lina." I rose to stand, leaning her backward so as to fuck her face. I needed to fuck her face.

Her mouth so warm and wet around me, tears at the corners of her eyes from trying to take my length, my thickness.

And with her on her knees before me, her mouth stuffed with my cock, knowing I shouldn't, knowing I should stop, I thrust deep into her throat and heard her choke as I came. As my dick throbbed and I came down her throat in ecstasy like I've never felt before, the thought of her swallowing my cum almost too much to bear.

When it was finished, I drew out just a little, just enough for her to breathe. She'd been pushing against my thighs. I felt it now. I stood like that, head bowed, holding her, feeling her little tongue on me. When I opened my eyes, I found her looking up at me and fuck, seeing her like this, naked and with my cock still stuffed in her mouth, I could get hard all over again.

But I slid out of her and tucked myself back into my pants.

One time. Just once. It would never happen again. I just...I needed this now. Fuck. I wanted her. I wanted her so badly. I always had.

Drawing her up to stand, I kissed her mouth still wet with my cum, tasting myself on her, tasting her, sliding one hand between us to cup her dripping cunt.

Walking her backward to the bed, I pushed her to lie on it, her legs dangling over the side. I shoved them apart and knelt between her knees and, drawing her pussy open.

God. I could look at her like this forever. I did for a long time.

I feasted first with my eyes, then with my mouth, licking her length from hole to hole, hearing her gasps, feeling her hands fist my hair when I sucked her hardened clit until she whimpered, calling out, pulling me hard to her, wrapping her legs around my neck, and coming on my tongue, bucking with it as she panted my name.

5

LINA

We lay in bed, neither of us saying a word for a long time, maybe both of us wondering what the hell had just happened. At least, I was pretty sure that's what was going through Damon's head.

Me? I wanted it. I'd always wanted it. Wanted him. From that day we'd spent together four years ago, I'd wanted him. It wasn't even just sex. I just wanted to be with him.

I'd never believed in love at first sight, and that wasn't what this was. It was deeper than that. Like two souls who belonged together were finally coming together. It made no sense. Even thinking it made me feel like an idiot, but that was it.

Damon held me to him, his arm draped over me. I had my back to him, his legs bent behind mine, his nakedness against my nakedness. I listened to him breathe. And I could feel the guilt rolling off him.

"I meant to punish you. Only punish you."

I swallow.

"But fuck. Fuck me."

He sat up, swung his legs over the bed and switched on the light. I drew the covers up and looked at him, watch as he pushed a hand into his hair, expression heavy.

"It can't happen again. It won't."

I opened my mouth, but he picked up his discarded clothes and walked away, went to the bathroom. There, he turned.

"Get dressed. I'll take you home."

He closed the door behind him. A few minutes later, I heard the shower go on.

I sat up and shook my head, confused.

Hurt.

He regretted it. And he was in there washing me off him.

Shoving the covers off, I dressed quickly and grabbed my coat and purse. I paused then, glancing at his wallet on the table. I had no money. I needed to get home, and I had no money. Alexi controlled everything. No. I couldn't think of Alexi now.

Feeling like the lowest of the low, I opened his wallet and took out a $50 bill. I slipped out of the room, ran down the stairs, and out the door, where I hailed a taxi. I climbed in and gave the driver my address. I didn't look back as the cab drove away, wiping stray tears away instead.

What had I expected? A declaration of love?

Why had he done it? Why had he even started it? He had no business starting something he had no intention of finishing.

My cell phone rang a moment later. I reached into my purse to take it out. Damon. Of course. I didn't answer. I didn't want to talk to him. I sent a quick text, knowing he'd come after me if I didn't.

"I'll save you a trip. I'm in a taxi heading home. I don't want to see you again, Damon. And I'll assume you won't say a word to Sofia about having run into me, considering. Have a good life."

Then, feeling guilty about the money, I sent a second text.

"Borrowed money for cab fare. Forgot my wallet. I'll send you a check."

I switched it off, knowing he'd call again.

When I arrived at the brownstone, it was a little after two in the morning. I paid the driver and climbed out, feeling a momentary panic that Alexi was back in town. He liked to drop by unexpectedly. Fucking jerk. I don't know why he bothered. It wasn't like I was ever going to give him what he wanted.

The day his father, Sergei, had been arrested, he'd transferred the club's title to Alexi. I didn't understand why but was sure it had to do with the charges and with protecting assets. I knew who

Sergei Markov was when I first came to New York. I'd sought him out. I knew the kind of business he ran, the things he'd done. But he'd been different than I'd expected. And to me, he'd always been kind.

Maybe I was blind, or desperate, but he'd accepted me, and in a way, he'd taken me in. Back then, I'd needed that more than I realized. Maybe growing up with a cold substitute for a father had done that to me. Had made me willing to overlook terrible things.

He'd lent me money to get set up when I'd first come here. He'd also let me live in the apartment until I found something else. Thing was, I'd never been in a rush to move out. He claimed he wanted me there—better than leaving it empty, he'd said—and I had accepted the offer, always telling myself I'd look for something else soon.

When Sergei was arrested and Alexi stepped into the picture, though, everything changed.

Alexi had accused me of stealing from his father, of seducing him and tricking him into giving me money, a place to live. He'd made me an alternate offer. Fuck him, and he'd treat my loan like any bank would. Don't, and pay him back at an exorbitant interest rate, which he and I both knew I'd never be able to do.

Since I didn't take him up on his first offer, he insisted I stay on at the club and in the apartment, claiming he needed to be sure he got his money back. When I'd made the mistake of reminding him it was his father's money, he'd slapped me so hard, I'd needed makeup to cover the bruise on my face for more than a week. His private bodyguard, Maxx, had been there. He'd caught me when I'd fallen, but he'd made no move to protect me. Instead, he'd stood me back up, so I could take more.

Alexi hadn't hit me again, though.

He'd repeated his offer. I'd politely declined him again and agreed to the arrangement. Now, I worked—essentially for food—because he skimmed so much off my paycheck that I barely had enough to get back and forth to the club.

I knew all along it wasn't about money. Alexi hated his father. He wanted Sergei to be crucified. Because only then could he take over the family business. The fact that I had a special relationship with his father baffled him. I still wasn't sure he believed it wasn't sexual. His small brain couldn't process a relationship based on anything else, I guess.

I wasn't even sure if he wanted me because he was attracted to me or to take one more thing from his father. I did know, however, how dangerous Alexi Markov was. And the thought of Damon crossing his path scared the crap out of me.

A glance up and down the street told me he wasn't there. Maxx usually waited outside in his ridiculously oversize SUV, sometimes blocking the street like the dick he was while Alexi was inside.

Breathing a sigh of relief, I fished out my keys and went into the building, up the flight of stairs to the second floor, and into my apartment. After closing the door, I slid off my coat and shoes, set my purse on the table, and switched on the light.

The moment I did, I let out a small scream.

"You're going to wake the fucking neighbors."

Alexi sat in the center of the couch in the dark, arms spread wide across the back of it, looking pissed off.

"Shit, Alexi. You scared the crap out of me!" Best to act like nothing was out of the ordinary.

"Where were you?" he asked, rolling his r's. He'd grown up in some small Russian town, and no matter how long he lived here, his accent lingered. Strangely enough, it was worse than Sergei's, but that's probably because Sergei hadn't found out he even had a son until Alexi was ten. He'd brought him to the States then, but the accent stuck.

I went into the kitchen to get a bottle of water, not wanting him to see my face. "Getting drinks with a girlfriend."

"You don't have friends."

I leaned my back against the counter, staying in the kitchen and watching him through the opening at the bar. "I have friends."

"Who?"

"The girls I used to work with." Before working at Club Carmen, I'd waitressed at a cheap motel restaurant for all of five weeks. I'd hated every minute of it, but it paid for my cot in the apartment I shared with six others. The conditions had been awful, but it was better than this, wasn't it? Better than having to answer to a mobster who hated me. "I was wound up after work, so I went out there, and we had some drinks. That's all. Why do you care, Alexi? Why are you here sitting in the dark?"

He rose to his feet. My heart raced as he approached, and I wondered if he'd smell sex on me. If he'd smell Damon on me.

My chest tightened at the thought of Damon.

Alexi came right up to me, the toes of his shoes pressing against my bare feet. I hadn't bothered to put my stockings back on before leaving. I'd just wanted to get out of there before the humiliation of having Damon take me home. Alexi now stood close enough that I felt his body heat and hoped my face didn't betray my panic.

He looked me over slowly, his gaze settling on my lips for a moment. He then inhaled deeply.

"I smell a lie, Kat."

Kat. I'd forgotten he called me Kat. I'd become Lina again, the very moment I'd seen Damon.

"Liars tell lies," he continued. "I don't like liars, you know that, don't you?"

"Your sense of smell is off," I said, somehow

sounding a thousand times more casual than I felt. I stepped around him and went into the living room to look through the mail I'd stacked on the coffee table. "I'm not lying." Dropping the envelopes back on the side table, I faced him. "Listen, I'm tired. It's been a long night. What can I do for you, Alexi?"

At that he grinned. "You can take off that dress for starters." For a moment, I wondered if he actually thought he had a chance with me. If he thought I was remotely interested. But then his expression changed. "You know you're supposed to leave those dresses at the club. Uniforms aren't personal property."

"Are you serious?"

He stalked into the living room and stood just close enough that I knew how much bigger than me he was. How much stronger. How much more dangerous.

"Those are designer. They're expensive. You can't afford to damage one and have to owe me even more than you already do, can you?"

My jaw tightened. This wasn't about the dress. It was about humiliating me.

"Can you, Kat? Can you afford to owe me another penny?"

"No."

"Take it off."

I took a step to walk into the bedroom and change, but he grabbed my arm.

"Here."

I studied his cold eyes, blue, like Damon's, but so fucking different. Inhuman. Dead. I reached to take down the straps, pulled the dress off, and stepped out of it. Second time tonight. I held it out to him, not covering myself even though I stood in just a pair of panties. I wouldn't show him he'd won, that he'd humiliated me.

Alexi's grin widened, and he slowly dragged his gaze over me.

"The panties are mine," I said, breaking into his power play. "Take the dress and go. I need to get to bed."

His eyes narrowed, and as he reached to take the dress, he gripped my wrist. "Offer to work a party still stands," he said. "You'd be done paying me in a third of the time. And if you wanted to be done at once, well, you know what I require."

"No thanks. On both counts."

He released my wrist and walked away, taking his coat, which he'd hung over the back of a chair.

"Don't be so hasty to answer."

He opened the door but turned to look me over once more.

"You could make a lot of money, Kat. I know many men and women who'd pay handsomely to have you on your knees—"

"Get out."

"Are you kicking me out of my own house?"

He loved to lord it over me. "It's your father's house."

His mouth tightened, and his hand fisted. I needed to be careful.

"How's your sister, by the way? Belly swelling with those sweet, tiny little babies?"

I stared at him, anger turning to something else. Fear.

Swallowing my pride, I bowed my head. "I'm just tired, Alexi. Thanks for coming to pick up the dress I borrowed. I won't let it happen again."

That seemed to satisfy him because when I looked up, he was smiling victoriously.

"Almost forgot. There was a reason I dropped by. Leslie's sick. I don't think she'll be able to make the party tomorrow night. I'm going to need you to take her place serving."

"I told you, I'm not interested in working a party—"

"Relax. I'm talking about serving drinks. Not your pussy."

I guess it was shock at his language that silenced me, giving him that second he needed before I told him no.

"After your shift on piano." He reached into his pocket and withdrew his wallet, took out some bills, and tossed them on the table. "Make sure everything's taken care of, Kat. My guests pay for the cream of the crop."

I glanced at the bills on the table, feeling like a whore for the second time that night. Even if I wasn't fucking him, it's what everyone thought, wasn't it? His whore to display and humiliate.

"You're a good girl, Kat. You just need to learn when to bow down. I'll teach you. My father spoiled you, but I'll teach you yet."

We stood facing each other another moment before he finally walked out. I locked the door behind him, leaning against it, breathing hard. I hated him. I hated Alexi. I hated that I had gotten myself into this mess with him, because he wasn't ever going to let me go. He would always come up with something, some other thing I owed him. And the threat of hurting not only me but my family gave him power over me. There was no way out. Not until he tired of me.

I'd thought about giving in, about letting him have me, letting him get bored of me, but I couldn't. I just couldn't.

Would that even be enough anymore anyway? He wouldn't be satisfied until I crawled at his feet, kissing the underside of his shoe for all the world to see.

6

LINA

Did I expect Damon to chase me back to the apartment? Had I expected him to come the following morning? Because he didn't do either of those things. I turned my phone back on late the next afternoon to find I had four messages. I dialed my voice mail to hear Sofia on the first one.

"Hey sis. It's been a while. I know you're busy with school and all but give me a call. I'm bored to tears lying here all day. I hate bedrest. Hate it. Talk to you soon? Please? Pretty please?"

I smiled, but guilt quickly wiped that smile off my face. I'd been lying to Sofia for more than a year and I felt like a jerk about it.

At least I knew Damon hadn't told her about running into me. Was it because of my message the night before? Was he forced to keep my secret, now that last night had happened?

The phone went on to the next message. My heartbeat picked up when I heard his voice, deep and dark and worried.

"Lina. Fuck! You were supposed to wait for me to take you home. Answer your fucking phone. You know I don't like you out there on your own so late at night."

A few minutes later:

"We need to talk. Can't just bury your head."

A few minutes after that:

"Look, I have to go to Florida tomorrow. I'll be back in two days. I'm coming to see you then. It'll give us both a chance to think. Lina...I'm sorry about how things...I'm sorry I hurt you."

"Too late."

I deleted all the messages, regretting it the moment I did. But I wiped my eyes and got up. I had a party to attend tonight. Maybe Alexi was right. Maybe I should just work them, work these parties and pay him off.

I had options. I didn't have to whore myself out. I could serve drinks, like I'd be doing when covering for Leslie tonight. Or I could agree to his other offer. The one that would wipe out my debt in one night.

Public submission. Public punishment. Publicly being made to kneel. It wasn't like I knew these people. Although I wouldn't know if that was true. Guests wore masks.

The one party I'd attended had been months ago. He'd hired me as pianist and warned me I may see things that might shock me. Even his warning, though, hadn't prepared me for that night, and the few things I'd seen were from behind a gauzy screen separating me from the room. At least Alexi had made sure everyone knew I was off-limits, but would he do that again? Would he protect me again? And who'd protect me from him?

Damon.

No. No way. I had to get that thought out of my head before it ever took root there. Alexi already suspected something with me. If he found out about Damon, he'd hurt him.

I'd keep Damon far away from Alexi. And that was exactly why it was better for Damon to go away anyway. To not pursue anything. Hell, I should thank him. He was saving me the trouble of concocting more lies to make him leave me alone.

Later that night, I forced myself to eat dinner, even though I didn't have much of an appetite. I played to a full club but made several mistakes as I kept searching the crowd, hoping to see Damon's face. Hoping, stupidly, that he'd come for me.

My shift ended early, and another pianist, a man in his fifties, took over as I disappeared into the staff area. We all knew the private parties existed, and anyone who'd attended one in any capacity was made to sign a nondisclosure agreement, which also stipulated there could be no conversations about the parties between attending staff. We all just had to pretend they didn't happen. Pretend to un-see things that couldn't be unseen.

The parties took place in the penthouse of the building Club Carmen was located in. I made my way up at a little after eleven, following the instructions left for me in my locker to the letter: enter through the door designated for servers. Wash any makeup off my face and change into the uniform—which made me laugh.

By uniform, Alexi usually meant naked. Or almost so. The last time, servers had worn thongs to distinguish them from those available for use. You didn't want some guest mixing it up.

After changing, we were to wait in the designated room.

When I arrived, six others were already there. All but one were female. I got a glimpse of the uniform upon entering: a gold thong, a gold lace mask with eyes cut out, and gold platform pumps.

Oh goody.

I washed off my makeup and tried to pretend I wasn't standing in a room full of people as I stripped off my clothes, slid on my thong, and put the mask in place over my eyes. Another door opened, and two women entered rolling a table into the room between them. No one spoke. That was another rule. Absolutely no talking. I wondered what Alexi would do or how he'd even know if anyone broke that rule, but no one whispered a word.

The women started with the person closest to them, taking her to a corner that had been screened off. She stepped behind it, and we all watched that screen as silence permeated the room.

Ten minutes later, the girl reemerged. She looked stunning. Every inch of her was covered in gold from the top of her head to the tips of her platforms. She stood against a wall with her arms stretched out. I guess the gold they used had to dry. She looked ridiculous. But maybe this was part of Alexi's plan anyway. He liked the servants to know they were beneath him. That he could and would humiliate them at every turn.

The next girl followed, and we waited. I wondered about the single male server who had a face that was almost pretty. When it was his turn, he put on the platforms like the rest of us and went behind the curtain, emerging ten minutes later covered in gold. I was the last to go.

Behind the curtain, I stretched out my arms and spread my legs and the women painted every unmarked inch of me, working together like they'd done this a hundred times before. And when I was finished, I glanced at the mirror almost not recognizing myself. My tattoos remained untouched, and I knew they wouldn't go unnoticed in the next room. A special instruction from Alexi, I was sure. I would be wondering who'd seen me here every time I played piano at the club, and I already felt my face burn with embarrassment.

Music began to play in the main room, which meant the party had begun. I picked up a tray of filled flutes of champagne and followed the others out.

The room, much like the rooms at the club downstairs, were softly lit, a reddish tint that softened and made everything more beautiful. There were about seventy-five, maybe one hundred guests, and although one of the rules for servers was that we kept our eyes lowered, I snuck glances, unable to keep from looking at the masked faces, the elaborate, over-the-top dresses of the women, the sometimes frightening masks of the men. I felt gazes following me the whole time, and I may as well have been naked for all the thong covered.

Men talked, women giggled, drinks flowed, countless empty bottles of champagne stacked up in the kitchen. Then the groups started to form, small cliques holding private court in various alcoves or not so private ones in plain sight.

I wondered where Alexi hired his whores. Beautiful men and women to service all of his guests needs, however perverse. Soon, conversation muted to the sounds of flesh slapping against flesh, of moans of pain and of ecstasy. I tried to see only the marble floor before me, but felt people watching me at every turn. I searched for Alexi's icy gaze, knowing he reveled in my humiliation, but couldn't find him.

At a little after one in the morning, a gong sounded.

Everyone stopped. Someone clapped. Another cheered. The servers set their trays aside and lined up against one wall. I guessed they'd been given instruction to do so. I had not, but I followed them to it, taking a spot at the end of the line. Glancing at them, I saw how they'd not only lowered their gazes but bowed their heads. Clearly we were not supposed to watch whatever was coming next.

Men dressed in black poured in from two side doors and arranged chairs all facing the gong. People took their seats, looking more like vultures than ladies and gentlemen. The men in black disappeared, and now that everyone was seated, I had a clear view of what was happening.

The gong sounded once more, and quiet fell over the crowd.

I knew it was Alexi who walked to the center of the space from the way he moved. He wore black and had on a skull mask. I hadn't seen that one tonight but recognized the gold ring I'd noticed on a man earlier. It wasn't one he'd ever worn before, so I hadn't realized it was him. He must have swapped out the mask he'd worn earlier for this Grim Reaper's mask.

"Welcome, dear, honored guests."

He took a bow and switched to Russian then. I couldn't follow the speech but realized most of his guests did with the way they responded to him. At one point, the crowd erupted in hungry cheers. That was when Alexi stepped aside, and a door opened. A woman was led out by a man in black. He was also masked. She was dressed in an elegant black evening gown, her hair and makeup impeccable. The glance she gave Alexi was all that betrayed her trepidation.

Alexi switched to English, whether for the woman's benefit or not, I couldn't tell. I didn't want to think he did it to make sure I understood. Not given what followed.

"Nadia has agreed to the restitution I have laid out. She begs your forgiveness and is willing to take the punishment necessary to earn back your trust."

The crowd booed.

Alexi raised his hand to silence them.

"Nadia, show them how…repentant…you are."

Nadia glanced at him, then at the group. Her lip quivered as she reached to unzip her dress and let it drop to pool around her ankles. She wore nothing underneath. The hunger of the audience was almost palpable in their quiet as Nadia stepped out of her shoes and stood naked and barefoot before them.

The man who had led her inside returned with another dressed exactly as he was.

Between them, they carried a padded bench with leather straps across it. They placed it before the room and left.

Nadia glanced at Alexi, who nodded. She then moved to bend herself over the bench facing the guests, spreading her arms over the sides and her legs wide. Her chin rested on a raised upholstered shelf almost so she could look directly at the audience.

"Supplication is a beautiful thing, is it not?"

The crowd began to chatter.

"What say you? Five strokes to warm her before she's...opened up, so to speak. Ten?"

As he spoke, he moved to secure the straps over Nadia, one at her lower back which forced her ass higher, the other just beneath her shoulder blades, as two men worked to bind both ankles and wrists. All this while the audience called out yeas and nays. What the hell was about to happen? Why was he strapping her down, and what had this poor woman done? Was this some sort of game? Why would anyone allow themselves to be treated like this?

"Now, now. You'll all get your turn. Let's not act like barbarians, shall we?"

I watched from beneath my lashes as one of the masked men stepped forward, holding out a long, thin leather strap.

Nadia looked at it, tears on her cheeks as Alexi took the strap extended to him and circled her.

This was why he'd wanted me here tonight. Leslie hadn't gotten sick. He wanted me to see this. He hoped, no, he *expected*, me to acquiesce to something like this? To allow him to punish me like this to release me from my debt?

In the next moment, my gaze found Alexi's. He stared right at me, as if he were waiting for me to watch.

"Fine. Fine. Ten strokes it is then, and Nadia's body is yours to use for the rest of the evening. No limits. I personally can't wait." He raised his arm and, keeping his eyes locked on mine, he struck so hard, I jumped as Nadia let out a scream.

Alexi pulled his mask off his head and tossed it aside. His hair stood on end as he set his face and took aim before striking again, his lips tight with the ferocity.

Nadia let out another cry and tears streamed down her face. The audience watched in silence. I wondered if beneath their masks, they all wore grins. I'd bet they did.

Undeterred by her cries, Alexi delivered the rest of the ten then set the strap down on her back and smiled at the guests, sparing me one quick glance.

My heart raced.

He gestured for a man to open the door. He did, and a naked woman was led out on her hands and knees. Another woman, also naked, led her toward Alexi. There, she handed him the leash.

"Ah."

Alexi circled the woman, who remained on her hands and knees. He mentioned her name and had her stand to discuss various aspects of her anatomy. He then had her turn and bend over to the immense pleasure of the crowd. Once he handed the leash back to the woman who'd led her in, he began the bidding.

It was an auction. This was what he wanted from me.

The bidding began. The winner paid more than ten thousand dollars for the woman. I watched, shocked, as the woman was led to kneel along the wall and another one was brought in.

Altogether ten women and eight men were auctioned off for the night. I couldn't keep track of the amount of money that would exchange hands by the time the bidding was over and the real party began.

As the servers went to fill their trays with champagne, I followed, but Alexi called my name from behind. I stopped. I didn't turn around, not yet.

"Lovely, isn't she?" he said. "Come here Kat."

I turned to find him talking with a couple. They'd taken their masks off, and they watched me with hungry eyes.

"We noticed you right away," the man said.

I glanced at Alexi, not sure what was going on.

Alexi's gaze examined me slowly, pausing at my nipples tight beneath the dry gold paint. "Gold is your color," he said.

"I'd like to place a bid," the woman said.

My mouth fell open, and, panicked, I turned to Alexi.

He smiled.

"Not tonight, I'm afraid. Kat's...not quite ready for us, are you, Kat?"

I didn't answer.

"Soon though, I think. Very soon, I'm sure, in fact," he said. They moved away, dismissing me.

I stood watching them for a moment, then turned my gaze around the room. The sounds, the sights, the smells: sex permeated the space, every act —depraved or not—played out before my eyes, and the woman, Nadia, still cried out as guests lined up to strap her or to fuck her, most did both.

I took a step backward then turned, trying to block the noise. I went into the kitchen and stood in line to pick up a tray, looking at the clock. Two hours to go. Two more hours before I could leave this place, wash this stuff off me, try to forget the night. Forget what Alexi had said. No, promised. I had to find some way out of this. Alexi was playing with me, and I knew that soon, he'd take what he thought he was owed. Soon, he wouldn't wait for my permission.

"Block it out," someone said beside me.

It was one of the servers. She smiled and loaded her tray with glasses.

"You're new to the party, right?"

"Yeah."

"Just block it out. Think of the money. Easiest grand you'll ever earn."

"How do you do it?"

"Well, I don't have Alexi Markov watching me like a hawk." She winked. "He likes you."

We picked up our trays. "No, he thinks he has some right to me."

"Alexi Markov always gets what he wants. It's not like he's bad to look at. I'd do him." She chewed her gum, which she hid well because we weren't allowed gum, and walked to the exit. "But if you're dead set not to, keep a very low profile."

She walked out into the party room. I set my tray down, feeling sick to my stomach, and made my way to the bathroom, where I locked myself in, trying to block out the noises of the party.

I had to find a solution to this. I had to find some way to get Alexi off my back for good. I couldn't run or hide. I'd tried that once, and he'd found me within twenty-four hours. Besides, I didn't have the means to do it. He made sure of that. And there was more than my safety to think about. There was Sofia. Her babies. He'd mentioned them more than once. And this was not about a fuck. He wanted more than that. I'd become some sort of obsession for him.

Someone knocked on the door. "Just a minute."

They left. I looked at my face in the mirror, feeling like I couldn't breathe, when I heard Nadia cry out again. God, they weren't finished with her yet. I pulled at my hair. I had to get out of here. I couldn't be here one more minute.

I scrubbed furiously at the paint on my face and got dressed. I walked out of the bathroom and left the building as quickly as I could.

Snow had begun, the blizzard they'd predicted now a reality. I ran from there, stopping at the all-night liquor store a block from the subway station and buying a bottle of cheap whiskey. I wanted to be obliterated tonight. I needed to be out of my head.

I ran fast, habit somehow carrying me to the subway where I boarded my train, where, without being able to get the image of the Alexi's victorious grin out of my head, I got off at the right stop. I needed to get to the apartment before I lost it, lock myself in, even if I knew how pointless that was. I wanted to submerge myself in water so hot, it would melt the gold paint off my body. Burn the images out of my mind.

Alexi liked fucking with my head. He knew tonight would terrify me. The conversation with that couple? I had no doubt he'd set that up. He wanted me unhinged, scared as fuck. Well, I was. And I also had no doubt he'd be back soon to make good on his promise.

There was only one person who could help me. Sergei. But would he help me over his son? And if he didn't, and Alexi found out I'd gone to him? What then?

Underneath all this insanity, the image of Damon that night, his eyes, his face, the feel of him holding me, his arms around me—I wanted to lose myself in that memory. I wanted to let myself—for one fucking second—feel safe. Feel like I had some control of my life. Feel like I could breathe.

But I couldn't do that. I couldn't think of him. I couldn't think of him ever again.

7

DAMON

Lina didn't come back to her apartment until late the following night. Later than her usual shift at the club by several hours. She didn't see me when she turned the corner. For one thing, the streetlamp was busted so it was pitch-black. For another, she expected me to be in Florida, so she had no reason to look for me.

But I hadn't gone to Florida, not after that second text of hers telling me she'd taken money out of my wallet. Instead, I'd been standing here, freezing my ass off, waiting for her as snow fell.

I didn't care about the money. I just didn't like that she hadn't even had enough for a taxi to get home.

When I'd looked through the kitchen cabinets at her apartment, they'd been empty. In her refrigerator, she had water and eggs. She told me she ate at the club and made the excuse of not liking to cook, but there wasn't a single takeout container in the place. I wasn't sure I believed her, and I didn't like it. She couldn't weigh more than a hundred pounds.

She was in some sort of trouble. I had no doubt of that.

Lying about school had been one thing. I believed she needed space and time to heal after what happened with her grandfather, with the loss of everything. She probably blamed herself for turning over evidence.

Now things were different. I needed to figure out what kind of trouble she was in.

As her steps neared the house, I stood. A motion detector lit up the space. Lina stopped, clutched her chest, and stumbled backward, as if she'd turn and run. I took a step forward, so she'd see that it was me.

She'd been crying. I could already see it in her red, puffy eyes.

"What are you doing here?"

"It's good to see you, too."

"You're supposed to be in Florida."

"I postponed my trip."

She shook her head, as if having some discussion in her head, and walked up the stairs, brushed past me and slid the key into the lock. I didn't miss how her fingers trembled.

"Has something happened, Lina?"

She opened the door a little but stopped, dropping her head. "I don't want to see you, Damon. I told you. Leave me alone." She pushed the door wider and attempted to slip away, but I caught her arm.

"What kind of trouble are you in?"

She turned to look up at me.

I noticed a smear of gold across her cheek. Makeup?

"I have to go." She tried to tug free. I didn't let go. "Just respect my wish and leave me alone."

"You've been drinking. I can smell it."

She stood with her back to me.

"You have no idea how tired I am, Damon. Please just let me go," her voice broke.

"Are you drunk?"

"Not enough liquor in the world."

I turned her to face me. Tears wet the skin around eyes that were shadowed and dark. Like she hadn't slept in a long time. I saw more of that strange gold on a strand of hair that had fallen free of her hat. Reaching my hand up, I went to pull it off.

She placed hers over the top of mine. "Don't."

Ignoring her, I slowly drew the hat off. She didn't even fight me. Her hair was painted gold. Not only that, her neck too, and the backs of her hands.

"What the hell is this?"

She stared up at me, unwilling or unable to

answer. But I didn't need her to answer. I could guess.

"Please go away."

"No. I'm not walking away, Lina. I won't leave you to handle whatever this is on your own."

Her lip trembled, and her face fell, her eyes pools of water. She clutched the collar of my coat and pressed her forehead into my chest. A sob rocked her body.

I looked down at the top of her head, at her hair matted with gold paint, and I wrapped my arms around her and pulled her to me, smearing paint onto my coat as I held her. She cried for what felt like a long time, heavy weeping that made her tremble.

"Let's go upstairs," I said, taking the keys from her hand and lifting her in my arms. She was so light and she just kept her face buried in my chest.

I opened the apartment door and set her down. She walked directly into the bedroom. I followed to watch her stripping off her coat, dropping it on the floor. Her sweater was next, then her jeans. She was naked underneath, and every inch of her, every inch apart from the tattoos, was covered in gold.

"What is this?" I asked, my voice foreign even to me as rage began to boil my blood.

Without answering, Lina went into the bathroom, plugged the tub drain, and switched on water so hot, it steamed almost immediately. She stepped into the tub, flinching at the heat but forcing herself to stay. She lowered herself down. I stood in the doorway and watched her hug her knees as water filled the tub, a golden sea around her.

I took off my coat, rolled up my shirtsleeves, and went to her.

She wouldn't look at me. She kept her eyes closed. Silent tears rolled down her cheeks as the water reached the tops of her arms.

"What happened tonight?" I asked, adjusting the temperature. I reached down to unplug the drain and let the golden water wash away.

Her face wrinkled at my question, but she didn't answer, didn't move. She seemed unable to even lift her arms to wash herself.

I picked up the soap and washcloth and began to scrub the paint from her back, shoulders, and arms, rubbing harder than I needed to, wanting it gone, needing it gone.

"What happened?" I asked again, not wanting to hear her answer, knowing already where she'd been. Knowing this involved the Russian mobster's son.

I plugged the tub again once much of the gold had disappeared down the drain. When the water was deep enough, I took the cup on the edge of the tub and poured water over her head, then shampooed her hair, the gold sticky there. It took three shampoos before I got it all out. Three times of emptying the tub and refilling it, the hot water running out. All the while, she just sat there, letting me.

Only when every speck of that paint was gone did I stop. I knelt beside the tub and looked at her sitting with her arms wrapped around her knees, eyes downcast, her face, blotchy from crying, flushed from the hot water. I took her chin in my hand and forced her to look at me.

"Did he hurt you?"

She dragged her gaze to mine, confused for a moment, then looked at me as if seeing me for the first time.

"Not yet."

The relief I felt was short lived.

She reached her arms up, wrapped them around my neck and closed her mouth over mine, kissing me. It was as though she couldn't get close enough. As though she'd burrow right under my skin. Disappear there.

I kissed her back. I knew it was wrong even if it felt right. I knew I should stop, but I didn't. Not at first. I kissed her back, tasting her, remembering last night. Remembering her across my lap, then on her knees. Remembering laying her on the bed and spreading her legs to look at her, taste her.

"Fuck."

I groaned. Taking her wrists I drew her off.

"Damon."

"We can't," I say, my voice hoarse. Forced.

She looked at me with hurt in her eyes. But there were more important things right now. I needed her to talk. I needed to find out what we were dealing with exactly.

I stood, adjusted my dick because fuck, it remembered too.

She stood in the tub, water dripping off her.

I swallowed hard, looked her over, wanted her. "Just one kiss."

I wrapped my hands around her wrists, felt her naked body yield to me, making me wet as she molded herself against me. I released one wrist to cup the back of her head, kissing her harder, her lips soft and open, her taste like whiskey and need.

Fuck. I wanted her. I wanted to fuck her.

With a groan, I lifted her out of the tub, grabbed a towel and carried her into the bedroom to sit her on the edge of the bed. I wrapped the towel over her shoulders and looked at her, her eyes wide on mine as she clutched the towel to herself.

I exhaled, then sat beside her.

She misread my intention and turned to me, pushed her towel off her shoulders and straddled my lap.

"No," I said, taking hold of her arms. "We can't."

She kissed my face, then my mouth, her nipples grazing my chest, the soaked shirt the thinnest barrier but I didn't even want that between us.

"Stop. I told you this can't happen again."

"Why not?" she asked, her breath damp on my face, my lips.

"It just can't."

"Then why are you here?" she asked, her eyes closing when she kissed my mouth again.

It took all I had to not kiss her back, not to throw her down on the bed and lay my full weight on her and fuck her until I'd had my fill.

Gritting my teeth, I gripped her wrists and stood, forcing her to stand. "This is too fucking hard." I pushed her into the chair in the room. I needed to put distance between us. I found a discarded shirt on the bed and handed it to her. "Put it on."

She did, although reluctantly, and watched as I walked away, then back. I leaned over her and set my hands on the arms of the chair.

"Tell me what that stuff was. The gold. Tell me what it was for and where you were and what you meant when you said he didn't hurt you *yet*."

She shut down instantly, shifted her gaze to her hands, then began to pick at a cuticle.

"I can't help you if you don't let me," I said when she wouldn't look at me.

When she turned her face up, she gave me a strange sort of smile. "I don't need help. I'm not asking you for it."

"I think you do need help. I think you're in something that's way over your head."

"I was at a party, Damon. I worked a party."

My grip on the chair tightened but I needed to keep holding on. If I didn't, I'd shake her. Ask her what the fuck she thought she was doing.

"I worked one of Alexi's parties. They painted us gold. That's what that was, just some makeup. I'll get paid tomorrow. I'll return the fifty bucks I took from you then."

"This isn't about money, and you know it."

"Really?" She cocked her head to the side. "What's it about, then?"

Her face grew harder, eyes colder and completely closed off to me. That girl that I'd held in the bath, she was gone. She was so far gone I almost wasn't sure she'd been there at all.

With an exhale I walked away.

Lina pulled her feet up on the chair and when I turned back, I could see her sex peeking out from between her legs. Was it on purpose? Was that her intention?

I stood there looking for a long minute, my cock rebelling. It wanted her.

I shifted my gaze. The thought of her at a party, naked, painted gold for everyone to look at, it made me want to put my fist through the goddamned wall.

"What do you mean you worked the party?" I asked.

"What do you think I mean?" she asked. "You're right. I don't live here for free, Damon. I pay. Just not with money. I make myself available to Alexi. I let him parade me around. He likes the tattoos. I let him use me however he wants, and I get paid for it."

I watched her face as she said it, heard how cold and hollowed out she sounded.

"I don't believe you." I said, my voice low and hoarse, fists so tight my fingernails cut into my skin. "You told me…" I turned away, ran a hand through my hair, tugging it hard before facing her again. I went to her, took her by her hair and pulled her to her feet.

"You're hurting me!"

I didn't let up. Instead I made sure she didn't look away from me. "You told me you don't do that for him. You told me."

She tried to grin, but I twisted my fingers and wiped that grin off her face.

"I lied," she said. "I lied about that like I've lied about everything else. You just don't want to see it."

I searched her face. Watched the tears that collected at the corners of her eyes.

"You're lying now." I released her with a jerk, tossing her onto the bed.

"You want to spank me again, Damon? You want me to bend over the bed? Maybe use your belt? Really teach me a lesson. Just be careful," she goaded. "Maybe you won't stop at licking my pussy this time. Maybe you won't be able to resist fucking me."

I counted to ten, focused on my breathing. She

was goading me. She was hurt. And she was young. I needed to remember that.

"How do you want me?" she asked.

She walked around to the foot of the bed. She dragged her gaze over my chest to my jeans where a half-blind person would see my erection. She came to me, closed her hand over the buckle of my belt.

"How do you want me?" she asked again, this time, sounding on edge, hard, but also broken. Like a broken little doll.

I covered her hand. "Don't do this."

"How? Tell me."

"Stop. Lina, stop this." What in hell had happened to her?

Red rimmed her eyes. "Why?"

"Because this isn't you." I shoved her out of my way. "You're drunk, and this isn't you."

"It is me! That girl you knew? Lina? She's gone, Damon. Long gone. It's just Kat now. This is exactly me." Her face crumpled momentarily but she blinked, forcing that weakness away. It didn't matter though. I'd glimpsed that vulnerability.

"How much did you drink tonight?" I asked. She didn't need me to be soft with her. Not now. She didn't even want it.

She shrugged a shoulder and turned away.

"Where's your purse?" I didn't wait for her to answer. She'd dropped it on the floor in the bedroom. I opened it and took out the half bottle of whiskey. "Please tell me you didn't drink all this tonight."

"What's it to you?'"

"Fuck, Lina—"

"Fuck Lina's about right. But if you're not going to fuck me, then get out. Why don't you ask me if I liked it," she taunted.

"Shut up."

"Ask me. Ask me if I liked everyone watching me."

"Goddamn it, I said shut up." I gripped her arm and stripped the covers off the bed, then tossed her onto it. As soon as I stepped away, though, she sat back up.

"Lay down," I ordered, my voice low and quiet.

"I thought you'd prefer me bent over."

"Shut up and lay the fuck down. You're going to sleep this off."

"Make me shut up. Make me. Make me lay down."

"Is that what you want?" I looked down at her and stepped closer, looming over her so that she had to tilt her head way back to see me. I was just pissed off enough to do what she asked.

Her eyes grew wide as she leaned back a little. She didn't speak. Nice change.

"You want me to make you?" I unbuckled my belt. Her eyes locked on it as I tugged it free of my jeans with a whoosh. "This what you want?" I asked her, flipping her onto her belly, lifting her shirt up to bare her little ass.

"Damon—"

"Sobers you up pretty quickly, doesn't it?" I climbed on the bed and straddled her hips, denim the only thing between her soft ass and my hard dick. I took her arms, drew them over her head wound my belt around her wrists and through one bar of the headboard, securing her to it.

"What are you doing?" she struggled, but it was done.

I got off her, and she turned to watch as I went into her closet and returned a moment later with two scarves.

"Damon."

I tugged one of her legs out to the right and secured her ankle to the footboard.

"What are you doing?"

She struggled, but I took her left leg and pulled it wide, too, before binding it too.

I stepped back to look at her lying prone on the bed, bound, spread wide—fuck, it hurt my cock to look at her, at her bared ass, the slit of her sex. I hadn't needed to do that. Hadn't needed to bind her *like that*.

I forced my gaze to her face and told myself I'd put her on her belly so if she vomited, she wouldn't choke on it.

Lie.

I unbuttoned my wet shirt and took it off, looked her over once more spread like she was. I picked the blanket that had fallen to the floor up to cover her but not before I gave her ass a hard smack.

"Ow! Fuck you."

"By the way, I will take you up on your offer later, *Kat*. I'd love to whip your ass. I think you need it. But I want you sober so you feel every lick of my belt." I walked to the doorway. "I'll be on the other side of this door. You just holler if you need anything. Get some sleep."

I took the half-empty bottle of whiskey with me and pulled the door closed, her cries of "you can't do this" and "you can't leave me here like this" making me smile a little.

After taking a sip of the cheap whiskey, I dumped the rest down the drain then settled on the couch for a short night's sleep. The only thing that made me feel better was knowing she was going to be hurting tomorrow after the bullshit of tonight.

8

LINA

I woke up to a sudden burst of bright light and someone yanking the comforter off me. My head throbbed, my mouth felt like it was stuffed with cotton, and my eyes like they were sealed shut with glue.

"Rise and shine, sweetheart. You've got a flight to catch."

I peeled my eyelids open and squinted in the bright light. Damon stood at the window, watching me with a satisfied grin on his face. I strained to see why it was so bright and realized the skies had cleared and sunshine now reflected off what looked to be a foot of snow. The blizzard.

"Headache?"

He walked over to me. I tried to sit up but couldn't pull either my arms or legs free. I glanced back at myself, seeing the blankets askew, one naked leg exposed. I remembered the night before. How he'd bound me to the bed. Why he'd done it. All the things I'd said.

"Always takes a few minutes for the memories to come flooding back, doesn't it?" He sat on the side of the bed, undoing one ankle, then the next, before coming to the head of the bed. He waited until I looked at him before reaching down to untie my wrists.

Heat flushed my cheeks. "What time is it?"

"Seven. Get up, have a shower. I'll pack your things."

"Pack my things for what?" My head felt like a bowling ball.

"We're going to Florida. I have meetings, and I'm not leaving you here alone. Not after last night."

I rubbed my sore wrists. "I can't just take off to Florida. I have a job."

"That's exactly the problem."

"Damon, I can't not show up."

"You'll call in sick. It's two days."

He got up and opened my closet, taking out a duffel bag.

"I can't call in sick," I said. I couldn't. For so many reasons, the least of which was the actual job. If I didn't show up at Club Carmen tonight, Alexi would be here to figure out why. Well, if he wasn't on his way already after last night when I left the party before it was over. Before I was allowed to. Shit. "You have to go, Damon." I forced myself to move, swinging my legs over the side of the bed, clutching my head. I needed Advil.

"I'm going. We're going. Together. Taxi will be here in about twenty minutes, so get up and shower."

I walked into the bathroom and opened the medicine cabinet to find the bottle of Advil. I swallowed two with a handful of water.

"Listen." I came back into the bedroom to find him going through my dresser drawers. "About last night, I'm sorry. I was drunk."

Fishing out a handful of panties, he glanced at me before shoving them into the duffel. "I know you were drunk. We'll talk all about it later. Do you have a bathing suit?"

"I'm not going, Damon. I can't."

He stopped and looked at me. "You smell like a distillery after that whiskey. It would be nice if you would shower. For me and the other passengers."

I shook my head. "You're unbelievable." I turned and walked into the bathroom, the thought of Florida, of warmth and sunshine, a few days out of Alexi Markov's grasp, already warming me from the inside.

"We're short on time, so make it quick."

I stepped into the shower. Could I go? What would Alexi do? I'd call him once I got to the airport. He was going to be pissed anyway. He already was, I was sure, after last night. What could he do? Fire me? Kick me out of this apartment? Fine. Please. Set me free.

Damon walked into the bathroom, holding a pair of jeans and a sweater. "You can wear these. Let's go." He checked his watch.

I switched off the water, grabbed a towel, and wrapped it around myself. He stood in the doorway watching me.

"Why aren't you gone after last night?" I asked. "After what I told you. How awful I was to you."

He stepped up to me and brushed a strand of wet hair off my face.

"I told you I wasn't leaving you alone to handle this. We're going to go away, and you're going to tell me exactly what's going on, and then we're going to fix it. Get you out of whatever you've gotten yourself into. Together. I care about you, Lina. I'm not about to walk away and let you destroy yourself."

I searched his face, his eyes. It was like we'd known each other forever. It was like no matter what, no matter how awful I was or how badly I fucked up, Damon would be there, and that was that.

"It wasn't true," I said. "Last night, what I said, I lied."

"I know."

"It's better if you're not involved," I felt the heat of tears but managed to contain them.

"That's not up to you. It never was, not since the moment I walked back into your life."

"Damon—"

He put a finger over my lips to quiet me. I swallowed, his touch soft, leaving me wanting so much more. My chest tightened as we stood looking at each other, and I knew in that moment that I loved him. I loved Damon Amado. I think I had since I first met him.

And he was the one man I could never have.

But we could have *this*.

We could have two days, couldn't we? It would break me, but we could have it.

Stolen time.

Could one steal time? No. It didn't work that way. There was always a price to pay. But I would. I'd pay it.

A car honked its horn outside, and Damon dropped his arm. "That's the taxi. Get dressed, and we'll go. We'll stop at the church to pick up my things. Do you need anything else?"

I glanced around. "Sunscreen?"

He smiled. "We'll get that there."

A few minutes later, we walked out of the apartment and into the idling taxi. When we got to the church, I waited in the cab while he went up to get his things. I dialed Alexi's office line at Club Carmen, knowing he wouldn't be there yet, and left a voice mail to say I'd be gone for a few days. I didn't say more than that, knowing he'd be by to check the apartment once he got the message anyway. I hung up and switched my phone off as Damon returned, loaded a duffel bag into the trunk, and climbed back into the cab.

DAMON HAD church business in Miami, and the hotel he'd booked was just a block from the beach. I'd never been to Florida. The warmth in contrast to the icy, wet cold of New York City felt better than I could have ever imagined it could.

When we arrived, we took a taxi to the hotel. At check-in, when the desk agent mentioned it was a room with a king-size bed, he said that was fine. I was surprised, thinking he'd ask for two doubles, since he seemed determined that nothing would happen between us. I knew he was struggling against himself, wanting it, wanting me, as much as I wanted him.

"I've canceled my evening meeting, so I'll be back by three. You'll be on your own until then."

"That's fine. I think I'll lie down and take a nap. My head still hurts. Then maybe we can go to the beach together after?"

"I don't care where we go, but we need to talk. I need you to come clean with me, Lina. That means you tell me everything."

I nodded, but I couldn't commit to that. It was for his own protection.

"Make sure you eat something. Just charge it to the room."

Embarrassed, I nodded and looked away.

"And pick up sunscreen from the gift shop if you go out."

"You know I've been living on my own for two years, right?"

"I know," he said, taking some money out of his wallet and setting it on the desk. "I kind of sprung this on you, so I feel responsible."

God. So freaking embarrassing. "Thanks."

Our room overlooked the water. After Damon left, I decided I'd nap on the beach instead of in the hotel. I unpacked my things, put on my bikini and a sundress, grabbed a towel and my purse, and headed out. I'd relax and enjoy the next few hours and not think about anything. I'd need to face it all soon enough anyway.

After buying sunscreen, a straw hat, a pair of cheap sunglasses, and a magazine, I headed to the beach, slipping off my flip-flops as soon as my feet hit the sand, loving the feel of the warm granules between my toes, loving the heat of the sun on my shoulders. Finding a spot, I laid my towel down and stripped off my sundress, lathered myself with sunscreen, and took out my phone. I just needed to send Damon a message, telling him where I was.

I regretted it the moment I did as text messages loaded one after another on my screen. All from Alexi. Each one more pissed off than the last. I only read the ones I couldn't clear away fast enough, ignored the rest, and sent a quick text to Damon, telling him where on the beach I was and that I was switching off my phone. I then lay back, put my hat over my face, and closed my eyes.

When I woke up, it was to the feel of someone rubbing sunscreen on my back.

Startled, I sat up to find Damon by my side, smiling.

"You were burning."

"Oh," I looked around, remembering where we were. "I fell asleep. What time is it?"

"Four o'clock. My meeting ran over."

"Four? Wow. I've been out for hours."

He moved behind me and began to rub my shoulders, arms, and back with sunscreen.

"How long ago did you get the tattoos?"

"I've been getting them over the last year and a half. It's a process. You like them?"

He nods. "Did it hurt much?"

"Like a motherfucker."

He laughed. "And you used to be so sweet."

I liked his teasing. He capped the sunscreen and looked out at the sea.

"You know what I want?" I asked.

"What?"

"I want to forget everything just for the couple of days we're here. I just want to enjoy this. Forget New York City, forget the club, forget everything for a little while."

"We need to talk about it. You can't put it off forever."

"I know, and we will. Just not yet. Please."

He looked at me like he was about to tell me no. I stood and held out my hand.

"Swim with me?"

We spent the next few hours swimming and lying in the sun. Although tentative around each other, I don't think either of us wanted to spoil the mood between us. It was just as I'd thought. Like we'd stolen time, just a few days, and we both knew it.

After swimming, we went back to the hotel. As I climbed out of the shower, I heard Damon talking. I wrapped a towel around myself and walked out of the bathroom. He stood by the window, hand in the pocket of his pants, his hair still damp from his shower. When he heard the bathroom door open, he turned around, smiled, then put a finger to his lips.

In the next sentence, I heard him say his brother's name.

He was talking to Raphael.

I tiptoed to my duffel bag and fished out the skirt and tank top he'd packed for me. When I stripped off my towel, I watched him from the corner of my eye. He didn't turn away but remained watching me as he continued his conversation. He wanted me. And maybe it was selfish, but I didn't want to make it easy for him to resist.

Once dressed, I went into the bathroom and combed out my hair. I'd dyed it darker when I'd moved to New York. I liked the near black. It set off my eyes. I'd already picked up some color from the afternoon on the beach, and the bridge of my nose was a little sunburned, but I looked healthier for it. And I felt better. I knew it wasn't the sun's warmth that caused the latter. It was Damon's.

A few moments later, he hung up the phone.

"You didn't mention me," I said, keeping my eyes on the bathroom mirror as I combed out my hair and towel dried it.

Damon appeared behind me. "Not yet. But—"

"I know." I turned to him. "It's not right, and I will tell Sofia myself. Just give me Florida."

He nodded and looked me over. I did the same to him. He wore a blue T-shirt and jeans, his tan even deeper since this afternoon.

"How are you more tanned than me?" He'd spent not half the time out there as I had.

He smiled "You'll catch up tomorrow. Although" —he paused and ran a finger over my nose. "You're a little burnt." He studied me for the longest time. So long I felt my cheeks burn. "You're very beautiful, Lina. And very bad for me." With that he turned and walked to the door. He opened it. "Ready?"

"Just let me get my purse," I said, out of breath at those words. At the way he'd looked at me.

We walked out and grabbed a taxi. Damon had a restaurant in mind, and it took about fifteen minutes to drive there.

"This is cute." I looked around the small village-like shopping center.

"Coconut Grove. There's a tapas place I want to take you to. You like Spanish food, right?"

"I like all food."

He didn't hold my hand, but his fingers brushed my lower back as he led the way to Two To Tango, which was vibrating with life. Most of the restaurant tables were full both inside and out. People were laughing and talking, loud music played from the speakers.

The hostess confirmed his reservation and walked us to one of the outdoor tables, where misters kept the patio cool.

I sat down and looked around. Had he chosen the place for the food or to make sure it would be so loud and so busy that dinner wouldn't be an intimate affair?

"Like it?"

"Honestly I'd have preferred to stay in the hotel room and order room service."

"Lina—"

The waitress interrupted then to take our drink orders. Damon ordered a beer, and I ordered a frozen margarita. I was grateful she didn't ID me, but I could see her hesitation. I guess because Damon looked so much older she assumed I was too.

I wasn't ready for him to begin questioning me yet so I went first.

"Being in New York City, has it made a difference for you? Has it solidified your position one way or another as far as the church? Do you think you'll go back to seminary?" I asked, not caring that this wasn't the most private place. I had limited hours with Damon. I wasn't about to waste them.

"That's complicated."

"Not really. Are you happy?"

The minute I asked the question, it was like I heard it myself for the first time. It was those three words. Are you happy?

I felt my face crumple a little and my heart sink. I'm not sure if I succeeded at masking my emotions because I felt him watching me and he seemed to see right inside me. Right into my soul.

"Happy is hard, Lina. I'm content with many

things. Having my brother back home. Working together with him on the house. Seeing him happy with your sister. Knowing I'm going to be an uncle very soon. Those are all blessings for which I'm grateful daily. But am I happy? I guess I'd have to define happiness for myself before I can answer it."

"It sounds like a long way around to saying no."

"Might be. How about you?"

The waitress appeared with our food, plates and plates of tapas that she stacked on our table. My stomach growled at the sight and scent, and I picked up my fork as soon as she left. When I turned to Damon with my mouth full, I found him watching me. He was smiling.

"You're very different from when I first met you four years ago."

"I was sixteen." I chewed. "And ignorant of so many things." I didn't stop chewing and quickly forked up a shrimp marinated in garlic.

I'd come to terms with the oblivion I'd lived in most of my life. Understood why Sofia had kept certain things from me when Grandfather had made that arrangement giving her to Raphael as if she were a thing to be bartered and traded. That was in the past, and I could leave it there.

"Ignorance is underrated," Damon said.

"I agree."

"Answer my question."

"It was easier to be happy before."

He stretched am arm over the back of my chair, fingers on my hair.

"You never called me afterward. When I went back to Philadelphia," I said. I'd given him a note, telling him how much I'd enjoyed the day we'd spent together and asked him to keep in touch. I'd foolishly written down every possible way for him to do that. Thinking about my eagerness now embarrassed me.

"How could I? You were sixteen, and I was going to become a priest. You can see how there might be a conflict. The church doesn't need any more of that."

I knew that. But I'd been dumbstruck by Damon. "I grew up locked away in an ivory tower. You were the first man in my life, apart from Grandfather."

"Teenage crush."

"It wasn't that and you know it."

I could tell from his expression that he did. "Speaking of Marcus Guardia, what did you mean the other night? When you said there was one thing you hadn't told anyone about your grandfather?"

His abrupt change of subject took me by surprise. I put my fork down, everything suddenly so serious. So heavy.

"Whatever it is, I promise I won't turn you in," he said with a wink when I couldn't speak.

He chuckled at his own comment, but it took me a minute to understand what he meant. He was referring to my joke—that I could go to prison for tampering with evidence.

"I can't tell you that, Damon."

"What difference does it make?"

"Ask me something else."

He watched my face, his expression serious, considering, perhaps deciding whether or not to pursue this.

"When are you going to tell your sister the truth about the last year?"

I hadn't expected an easy question. There weren't any, not really. "Once I've figured out how to fix things."

"Lina—"

"Damon, I just need time. One day. Two."

"I'm not asking about the club or what's going on there. I'm asking about the fact you've left Chicago. That you're not in the city you're supposed to be in, not to mention school."

I raised my hand to get the waitress's attention. "Can we have another round of drinks, please?"

Damon sighed beside me as the waitress noted the order on her electronic pad. He reached under the table to squeeze my knee. I closed my hand over the back of his.

"And the dessert menu," he added.

I smiled at him.

"Sure thing," the waitress said as she cleared our dinner things.

"I'll give you Florida," Damon said once she'd gone. "Afterwards, you will talk to me. Tell me everything. Agreed?"

I nodded.

He turned our hands around so my palm was inside his and intertwined my fingers with his.

9

DAMON

When I'd decided to give Lina Florida, subconsciously, I was giving it to myself too. We'd have a space of two days out of time. Out of reality.

There'd be a price to pay, I wasn't fool enough to believe otherwise, but I did it anyway.

I had meetings most of the following day. By the time I got back to the hotel, it was dark and Lina was just coming out of the bathroom.

"Hey," she said, momentarily startled as she wrapped her hair in a towel, a bottle of lotion in her hand. "You surprised me."

I looked her over. She wasn't trying to be modest, and although I didn't think she calculated some grand seduction, I knew what she wanted. I wanted it too.

I should have asked for a second room, or at the very least two beds, when we'd checked in. The request had been on the tip of my tongue, but the girl had just given me the keys and I'd thanked her and taken Lina up to our shared room.

Sleeping next to her last night—fuck—I'd been hard the whole night and probably gotten about two hours of sleep, only finding relief in the shower in the morning. She'd worn one of my T-shirts to bed, and when I'd climbed in, she'd curled into my arms like it was the most natural thing in the world. And I hadn't pushed her away. I'd held her, smelling her hair, her skin, feeling her in my arms. Liking the feel of her there.

And all the while I'd lain awake, she'd softly slept.

Shaking off the memory, I held up a bag.

"What's that?"

"I saw it at a boutique nearby and thought it was your color." I handed it to her.

She looked at me with a strange, almost confused look on her face. Slowly, she took the bag and sat down with it on her lap. I suddenly got the feeling it had been a very long time since anyone had given her a gift. The thought of it bothered me.

Lina slowly drew the dress out of the bag. It was a pale, antique pink, knee-length, crocheted dress, simple and old-fashioned and very pretty.

"Wow. It's beautiful." She touched it delicately. "Really beautiful. Thank you."

"There are shoes to go with it."

She pulled the box out, opened it, and smiled. "Pink sandals. I never in my life thought I'd own pink sandals."

She stood and, dress in one hand, sandals in the other, she kissed my cheek.

"Thank you, Damon."

Fuck. What was I doing? "You're welcome."

"So we're going out then? We can do room service—"

I hadn't decided yet. When I'd bought the dress, I'd planned on taking her out. Dinner then maybe a walk on the beach. My intention was innocent.

But the road to hell is paved with good intentions. That's how the saying goes, at least. And I was no innocent.

"Take off the towel."

She swallowed, obviously not expecting that.

I stepped toward her, took the lotion from her. "Take it off."

Her hands trembled as she loosened her grip on the knot and slowly undid it, letting the towel drop to the floor.

I looked her over, her skin tanned from hours on the beach, her nipples hard beneath my gaze. The slit of her pussy shaved bare. I remembered how it tasted.

I leaned down, inhaled the scent of her hair, her shampoo. Opening the bottle of lotion, I poured some onto the palm of my hand and began to rub it into her, keeping my eyes on hers as I did, watching how her lips parted in surprise, listened to her breath hitch. I did her arms, her shoulders, walked around behind her and rubbed it into her shoulders and back, then walked around her again.

I crouched down to rub it into her thighs, my eyes level with her slit. I could smell her. Smell her arousal. I straightened, tossed the lotion onto the bed and sat on the edge of it. I ran a hand through my hair.

"Damon." Her face was flushed, pupils dilated.

This was wrong. So fucking wrong. But I could give us Florida. I could give us this. Couldn't I?

This sin.

What price would we be made to pay? And could I ask God to punish me? Only me?

What would this cost her?

I was older. I was supposed to be the responsible one. I knew better. I should stop. I should release her hand, force her to tell me the truth, do what I said I'd do. Figure out what was going on and help her. Get her out of the trouble she was surely in and let her go.

Let her go.

But I couldn't deny this thing between us. Not anymore.

"Show me," I said. I gestured to her pussy with my eyes. "Spread your lips and show me your pussy."

Her hands shook as she moved them to do as I said, and she spread herself open.

I looked at her, looked at her pink, glistening cunt. I wanted to lick it.

Wanted to sink my cock inside her.

I stood. "One night. Just one night." It would be the biggest mistake of my life, but I couldn't resist anymore. I wanted her. I wanted her more than I'd ever wanted anything in my life.

"One night," Lina repeated.

I pulled her to me, crushed my body against hers and kissed her. She felt so good. So fucking good.

"One night," I repeated as if that would make this any less wrong.

She kissed me back, and I wound my fingers through her hair, drew her head back, tugging a little harder than I needed to as I looked at her face. Her beautiful, open face. Watched as her eyes teared up at the pressure of my hand in her hair.

Shifting my gaze around the room, I walked her over to the desk and turned her to face it. "Hands stay here." I leaned her forward, placed her hands down on the desktop, and pulled her hair to turn her face to mine. Kissing her hard on the mouth, I met her gaze in the reflection of the floor-to-ceiling window, which now acted as a mirror.

Our room was on a higher floor but if someone looked up, they'd see us. It made this that much more exciting.

"Down." I moved behind her, pushing her forward with a hand between her shoulder blades, then nudged her legs apart. "Legs wide. I want to see your ass."

Standing behind her, I looked down at her prone body, then glanced at our reflection, watching her watch me. Watch us.

My cock like a steel bar I moved behind her, stripping off my shirt and tossing it aside before gripping her ass cheeks, kneading them, drawing them apart to expose her to me.

After one more glance at our reflection, I knelt behind her, keeping her spread wide.

Lina arched her back, offering herself to me. And fuck if I wouldn't take what she offered. What I so badly wanted.

"Your cunt is dripping, Lina."

She made a sound as I brought my face to her, inhaling her scent before licking the length of her, from her clit, over the folds of her pussy, to her ass, circling that tight ring, making her gasp before sliding my tongue back to her cunt.

Her scent, her taste, they were addictive. Like a fucking drug. Like *my* perfect drug.

She made me mad, insane with hunger, and I

ravished her. I licked her pussy and sucked her clit and tickled her asshole until her knees gave out and she dropped to the carpet and arched her back, face down as I finished her off, my dick about to tear free from my jeans as I licked her pussy and fingered her clit until she whimpered. Until she came.

I needed to fuck her. Christ. I was going to blow in my jeans if I didn't fuck her right fucking now.

I drew back and she turned to face me. We knelt as I kissed her, tongue on tongue, sharing her taste. I cupped her sex between us, and she clutched my shoulders.

"Let me taste you, Damon," she begged. "Please."

I undid my jeans, pushed them and my briefs down only as far as I needed to.

Lina, like a good girl, bent deep, her ass reflected in the window as she took me into her mouth and swallowed my dick. I took her by the hair to guide her, watching her like this, mouth full of me.

But I didn't want to come down her throat tonight.

I wanted to come in her cunt.

"You're so fucking beautiful with my cock in your mouth," I told her, drawing her off.

"I want—"

I shook my head, stood and dragged her up with me. "I want to be inside you."

She swallowed and watched me strip off the rest

of my clothes. I lifted her, lay her on the bed and climbed between her legs, taking them and pushing them wide so when I looked at her, I had a full view of her pussy and her asshole.

I brought my cock to her pussy, and she bit her lip as I slid into her tight passage. Not a virgin, but tight as hell.

"Fuck, Lina." I groaned, closing my eyes to feel her for a minute before opening them to watch her stretch to take me. "I like my cock in your tight little cunt."

I drew back, thrusting harder, knowing I'd hit that special spot when she closed her eyes and bit her lip, letting out a moan. I watched her, fucking her harder, feeling her fingernails digging into my shoulders as I took her, claimed her, made her mine.

"Damon...this feels...so good."

Lifting myself a little, I flipped her over onto her belly and hauled her hips up, pushing her head down. I twisted her hair, turning her so I could see the side of her face as I pushed a finger into her cunt then slid it and her juices up to her asshole.

"Oh, god," she started as I pushed my cock into her pussy and rubbed my finger over her asshole.

"Open. I want to feel your ass."

"I'm going to come again," she panted, closing her eyes just as the tight ring gave and I pushed my finger inside her.

I released her hair, gripped one hip as I watched

my dick drill into her cunt while I fingered her ass and when she came, when she moaned my name and her walls throbbed around me, I watched her face, her soft eyes as I came inside her, a low, deep moan emanating from my chest as I emptied inside her.

10

DAMON

I woke up to Lina's lips wrapped around my cock. With a moan, I touched her face, petted her hair. Kneeling between my legs, she moved her mouth along my length, her eyes on me as she did.

"Fuck. Me."

She pumped and sucked at once, her other hand between her legs.

Guilt gnawed at my gut. I was older than her and six months from being ordained. She trusted me. She was vulnerable. This was wrong. What I was doing was wrong. I should make her stop. I knew it. But fuck...

Reluctantly, I drew her off me and sat up.

"One night," I groaned. "We agreed."

"Florida," she said.

She knelt before me, her fingers still working her clit through her slick folds.

I couldn't take my eyes off her. I'd said one night, but we could have Florida.

"You're a dirty girl."

"Make me come, Damon. I want to come on your cock."

I watched her play with herself, watched her work her dripping pussy. I knelt up and pushed her backward, burying my face in her pussy. It took all of two minutes for her to come. I drew back, smeared her cum on my hand then moved her off the bed.

"Get on your knees," I told her.

She dropped to her knees before me, opening her mouth, thinking that's what I wanted. But I shook my head and fisted my cock, pumping.

"Not yet," I said. "Watch. Watch what you do to me."

She knelt, transfixed.

"I'm going to cover you in cum."

She licked her lips, her gaze shifting to mine momentarily before returning to my cock. She slid her fingers between her slit again.

I grinned, watching her. "You like watching?"

She nodded, darting her tongue out to lick the tip of my cock when I brought it to her lips.

"I like watching too. I like watching you finger your cunt."

"I'm going to come again, Damon."

"Dirty girl. Open your mouth and stick your tongue out."

She looked up at me, and I watched her. Saw how her face flushed, how she bit her lip as her eyes softened and she opened her mouth.

We came at the same time. Her on her fingers, me on her face, her tongue, her chest. I covered her in it and she knelt so obediently before me. So perfect.

11

DAMON

After showering, we ordered room service and ate breakfast by the window. It wasn't easy to put off the thoughts of earlier, of how wrong this was, but time was running out, and we needed to talk.

"I'm free until about lunchtime. Then you're on your own for the afternoon, but we'll have dinner together."

"Thanks for bringing me. I'm glad I came. Although I don't know if I really had a choice."

"Are you ready to talk."

She didn't quite nod, but she also didn't say no.

"I want to help you," I said. "I won't judge you, no matter what."

"I know."

"Why is this so hard?"

"Because I wish you didn't have to be involved. I

wish things were different, and just that we'd met again under different circumstances."

"Circumstances are what they are." I studied her, refilling my coffee cup as she held her mug and sipped hers.

"Do you know who owns Club Carmen?" she asked, following quickly with: "Shit. I feel like I just slammed us back into reality."

I felt the same way. "Up until a little while ago, it was Sergei Markov. Since his arrest, it's changed hands to his son, Alexi. The same man I saw you talking to a few nights ago. It looked to me like he made your skin crawl."

"Perceptive. You know who the Markov's are then?"

I nodded.

"The apartment I live in belongs to Sergei, not Alexi. Alexi just sort of inherited it or took it over when they arrested Sergei."

"Go on."

She bit her lip. "I didn't come across Club Carmen by accident."

"What do you mean?"

"I sought him out. I sought Sergei Markov out."

I waited, something telling me this was about to go from bad to worse.

"Do you remember when I mentioned that I had done something that could get me in trouble? That I had kept something back from Sofia and the investigators?"

"I remember, but..." I was confused. "I assumed it had to do with your grandfather."

"Well, when I turned over the journals that got Grandfather arrested, I...kept one."

"What do you mean, you *kept* one?"

She exhaled deeply, shrinking into herself a little. "He had ties to Sergei Markov. They'd done business together."

"What? Your grandfather and Sergei Markov?"

She nodded. "From what I understand, Sergei was interested in the Italian market, interested in taking it over from the Italian mob. I don't know much more. Grandfather's notes were probably only meant for himself to understand. He mentioned some names and mostly noted transactions with dates and dollars, some with initials and locations. There were just a few that were...more detailed."

"Lina, you have to hand that over to the authorities."

She shook her head. "My grandfather did bad things, Damon. Really bad things." Her eyes pooled with tears. "Worse than stealing money."

"Where's the notebook?"

"Hidden."

"Does Sergei know about its existence?"

She shook her head.

"How can you be sure?"

"I just know."

I studied her. Sergei Markov was too smart not to know. Didn't it explain his generosity with her? Didn't that explain why he kept her so close. To keep an eye on her?

"I still don't understand why you sought out Sergei Markov."

"I don't know. Or I didn't. Not then. I needed to believe Grandfather wasn't as evil as that journal made him out to be. I needed to see Sergei Markov for myself. I...I don't know. Maybe I needed to blame him. Maybe I thought it would exonerate my grandfather—in my mind, at least. I didn't really have a plan. I just needed to see him."

"Lina—"

"It's such a relief to tell someone."

She gave me a faint smile, and for a moment, I wasn't sure she understood just how dangerous her situation was.

"This is a Russian crime lord we're talking about."

"I know."

She quieted, biting the inside of her cheek, her forehead wrinkling as she shifted her gaze out the window.

"Go on, Lina."

She faced me again. "I only went to the audition for the pianist position at Club Carmen to see him. I never really expected to get the job. I didn't even really want it." She shook her head. "I don't actually know what I wanted, I guess. I didn't have a plan. But Sergei hired me on the spot, and... I don't know, I took the job. It was like fate was sending me a sign, so I took it. I got to know him a little bit. He was so different than I expected. I guess I'd thought he'd be a monster, but he wasn't. Not at all."

"Monsters come in all shapes and sizes."

"I needed to believe that my grandfather wasn't one. Finding Sergei was supposed to do that. To make me see that Sergei was the monster."

She exhaled and lowered her lashes. It took her a moment before she continued.

"He knew I was struggling financially and told me I could stay at the brownstone apartment until I found something else. He said it was empty. His last renters had vacated it, and he hadn't had time to look for anyone new. That's how I ended up there."

"You never looked for anything else? A place of your own?"

"I know I should have, but no, I didn't. I'd shared an apartment—rented a cot, actually—before I'd found Club Carmen. This apartment was nicer than anything I could afford. And it was free."

"Nothing is free, especially from a man like that."

She shifted her gaze to the side. "He also gave me an advance."

"This gets better and better."

"I'm telling you the truth, Damon," she snapped.

"Truth *you* asked for. You said you wouldn't judge me."

"Go on." I couldn't help the edge in my voice.

"Sergei was kind to me. Warm even. Warmer than my grandfather. And it was never anything sexual with him. He was more like a father. I even started to forget why I'd come to New York City in the first place. It was just easier that way. Easier to turn my back on the past, even though I knew I'd have to face everything at some point. Face what I'd done, the role I'd played."

"What about the journal? Have you considered turning it in?"

She shook her head. "I should burn it. I should already have burned it. It can only hurt Grandfather more, and I've done enough damage."

"You didn't do anything wrong."

She shrugged one shoulder. "Because of me, my grandfather is in prison. Because of me, we lost everything."

"No. Not because of you. He did that. Not you. And there would have been an investigation anyway, Lina. After the fire, before the insurance paid out, they'd have dug deep into matters. Who knows how much of this they'd have uncovered themselves."

"But the point is, they didn't. They didn't have to. I did it. And I did it because I knew what he had done to Sofia. How he'd sold her out. How he'd manipulated Raphael by using me. By threatening to not take me to my sister's wedding." Her voice broke. "What he made her do, it makes me sick, Damon." She wiped away stray tears and sat up straighter. "I guess I got it, finally. And then I realized he planned on hurting Raphael by stealing his family home out from under him. It was just so wrong. So awful. And the thing was, when I went to the wedding, I knew Sofia and Raphael would make it work, somehow. I could see it, see how they felt about each other, even if they couldn't admit it."

"If you know all this, why do you feel any guilt?"

"I don't know."

"Go on about New York City and the Markov's."

"Well, everything was fine, until Sergei got arrested and Alexi turned up. He made a new arrangement as far as the advance went. He started to take out what I owed his father from my paychecks, which he said I owed to Club Carmen, which in turn meant I owed him, and he tacked on an outrageous interest rate backdated to when I'd first received it. There was no way I could pay that back, and he knew it."

"How much are we talking?"

She looked down at her empty plate where she set her crumpled-up napkin.

"You have to understand, I had nothing—"

"How much, Lina?"

She met my gaze, and I knew it was going to be bad.

"A little over a hundred thousand dollars."

"A hundred-thousand dollars? Are you fucking kidding me? What could you need that much money for?"

"It wasn't all personal. Some of that—a lot of it—Sergei wanted me in designer dresses. He wanted me to go to hairdressers he chose, makeup artists, the works. I was his pianist—"

"You were his doll. His pretty little toy doll."

She opened her mouth, then closed it again. I saw the hurt in her eyes.

"Lina, you had to know he wouldn't just have given you that."

"I had nothing!" Tears reddened her eyes. "I'd come from having everything to nothing. I couldn't go back home. Hell, I *had* no home. I didn't want to go back to school. I just…I know it was stupid. I know how stupid I sound. How naive. I know." She rubbed the backs of her hands over her eyes. "Don't you think I know?"

I rubbed my face. This was worse than I realized. "That's why your cupboards are empty. Why you needed cab fare."

She looked away.

I continued. "Hence eggs and water."

"This is so embarrassing." She shook her head and looked out the window for a few minutes before continuing. "He took the dresses his father wanted me to have for when I played at the club, claiming they were uniforms. He accuses me of being his father's whore and won't accept the truth. He's jealous of his father. Hates him while at the same time, he's both desperate for Sergei's approval and terrified of his wrath. And I've become some sort of obsession for him. Maybe if I'd just have let him..." She glanced at me and stopped.

"I swear, if you had finished that sentence, Lina—"

"It's not even me he wants, Damon. Not really. I'm just something he can take from his father. Like he would steal a thing, a possession."

She looked off into the distance. When she spoke again, she was quieter.

"I'm sorry. I'm sorry for all of it, Damon."

"We'll go to the FBI."

"FBI? No. No way. They have informants everywhere. And you won't get involved. He'll hurt you. He'll hurt you to hurt me. Damon, he can't ever know about you."

My phone rang then. I glanced at the display. It was the seminary. Probably Gavin. I declined the call, but it rang again immediately. "I have to take this," I said, standing.

She nodded. I answered the phone. Lina sat quietly watching me, and I watched her as I listened to Gavin speak. It was as though we were in cahoots. She knew to be silent. To keep our secret.

When she got up to retrieve her phone from her

purse and sat down on the edge of the bed to scroll through messages, I turned my back.

"The meeting isn't until this afternoon," I said to Gavin. I had business here with a man whose annual donations to the seminary made things very comfortable. He needed to move the meeting up and, as far as Gavin knew, there wasn't a single reason why I couldn't adjust my schedule. I couldn't exactly tell him about Lina.

I ended my call and turned to her.

"I have to go."

"Already?"

I nodded. "The afternoon appointment can't meet with me when we had scheduled but has time now."

"Church business."

"Yes."

She nodded and busied herself with loading our breakfast dishes back on the room-service tray.

"Lina. I'm sorry."

"It's fine." It had to be fine.

She straightened and faced me. "You have no choice." Her voice came out stiff, her gaze accusing.

I took a deep breath in, slid my hand over to take hers, and turned her palm up to mine. My thumb rubbed a circle inside it. When I looked up, I saw the top of her head as she watched our hands together.

"I'll be back as soon as I can, and we'll continue talking then. We'll spend the afternoon together."

"This isn't going to make any difference, is it?" She met my gaze. "Any of this. Not for us."

Shit. "Lina—"

She shook her head and pulled her hand from mine. "One night. Two. We agreed." She shrugged a shoulder trying to appear casual. She was anything but.

"I'll be back. We'll talk then, okay?"

It took her a long time to answer. "Okay." She gave me the faintest smile.

Feeling like a jerk, I released her to pick up my suit jacket and slid it on. "You don't have to do this alone. I'm with you, Lina. I'll help you. I'm not going to let him hurt you."

I went to her, leaned down, and kissed her forehead. "I'll see you in a little bit. We'll talk through our options then. Just relax and enjoy the beach, the sun. Try not to worry, okay? We're going to figure this out together."

She nodded, biting the inside of her cheek again, and I knew it took effort for her to speak.

"Go. You're going to be late."

I knew I shouldn't go. The voice inside my head blared its warning to not walk away. Not walk out of this room. Because I knew if I did, she may not be here when I returned.

"I'll be back as soon as I can," I said. How could I sound so calm, so collected, on the outside when inside, chaos ruled my mind?

"Okay."

I took two steps toward the door, but Lina caught my hand. "I like you a lot, you know that, right?"

"I know. I feel the same." More. "We'll talk when I'm back."

I forced a smile and kissed her lips as a tear fell from her eye and skimmed my cheek.

12

LINA

I leaned against the door for a long time after Damon left, my heart feeling heavy, my stomach in knots. Last night had been amazing. These last couple of days the most beautiful of my life. Our attraction was electric, the sex intense, but it was more than that. Being with him, I felt safe. I felt at home.

But we were on borrowed time.

I knew my heart would break after Florida. I'd known it going in. Damon wasn't mine, not to keep at least.

I'd lied to him when I answered with an *'okay'* when he said he'd see me in a few hours. I wouldn't be here. I'd already made up my mind to go. I had to take care of my business, finish this thing with Alexi. Damon couldn't get involved. Alexi could never find out about him.

I packed up my things and dialed the airline to change my ticket. I'd leave now, go back to New York, finish this thing with Alexi. I could sort through the loss of Damon then, after it was done. I could feel what I had to feel after.

Damon would be pissed to find me gone, but I had to do it now, had to do it this way. Besides, he'd be gone all day. Maybe I could have everything straightened out by the time he got back to New York City.

Changing my flight was easy enough, and I promised myself I'd pay Damon back the fee the airline charged to his credit card as soon as I could. I grabbed a taxi to the airport, and by early afternoon, I was back in New York City, where the pristine snow of a few days earlier now looked like a gray slushy mess along the side of the road.

I checked my phone, but apart from Alexi's messages, there wasn't anything new. Damon didn't know yet that I'd left. I had a few more hours.

Not wanting to take a chance Alexi would be at my apartment, I didn't go there. Instead, I retrieved a card from my wallet and dialed the number to the car service before I lost my nerve. Sergei had put my name on the club's account as an authorized user when I first started working for him. When I called and told them who I was, it took them no time to tell me they'd have a car out to meet me at the airport in twenty minutes.

It wasn't long before the black sedan with its tinted windows pulled up. I waved, recognizing the driver from the few times I'd used the service. I'd always felt guilty to take advantage, opting to take the subway or walk instead. But Stanley had driven me every time I had used it, and I knew he was Sergei's personal driver.

After bringing the car to a stop, he climbed out and gave me a warm smile.

"Miss Kat," he said with his English accent.

Ever since Damon had come into town, I had to think twice when someone called me Kat.

"It's very nice to see you again."

I swear Stanley was about eighty and the politest man I'd ever met.

"Hi, Stanley, it's good to see you too." I almost hugged him but held back.

"It's been a long time," he said.

"I'm glad you remembered me."

"Mr. Markov wanted to make sure I take good care of you when you call. Hop in and tell me where you want to go."

I settled into the back of the warm sedan with its tinted windows, and once Stanley climbed in behind the steering wheel, I met his eyes in the rearview mirror and told him I wanted him to take me to the prison to see Sergei.

He didn't miss a beat, and if he thought it strange, he didn't say so. Instead, he nodded his head and began the hour and a half-long drive to where Sergei Markov was being held.

When Sergei had first been taken into custody, he'd added my name as an approved visitor. I still remembered when he'd called me to tell me he'd done that about two weeks after his arrest. I'd found it so strange, but he'd said if I ever needed anything, that I should come see him. I wondered now if he'd expected me to come all along.

Once we arrived, Stanley told me he'd walk me in as far as he could. I was grateful. I'd never been to a prison before, and the building with its tall double fences topped with barbed wire was formidable, to say the least.

"Terrible, isn't it?"

"Yes." I followed him. To my surprise, the guard at the first door greeted him by name. We walked through to another window, where he leaned in to talk to the woman behind the counter. She glanced at me, gave me a once-over, and told me I'd have to leave my purse, which I handed her. She gave me a claim ticket. She then pushed a button that buzzed another door open.

"Come on," Stanley said.

I followed, meek and quiet, too intimidated to say a word.

"Mr. Markov will be pleased to see you."

"Stanley, I'm confused," I started when we were

told to wait in a small room that contained a very old and worn sofa.

"About what?"

"I wasn't even sure they'd let me in honestly. Didn't think it'd be this easy."

"Mr. Markov has as many friends as he does enemies and as much influence even from here," he said with a wink.

A buzz announced another door opening before I could process that.

"This way," the guard said.

I got up, but Stanley remained seated. "Aren't you coming?"

"I'll be here when you're finished."

"Um...okay. Thanks."

I followed the guard down a long narrow hallway and into a room on the right where six tables were arranged in three rows. Each table had four metal chairs on either side. A vending machine with candy and another one with sodas stood at one end, and the walls, ceiling, and floor were painted a drab beige.

The guard pointed to a table. I took a seat and waited. A few minutes later, a door opened, and a guard entered, followed by Sergei, who was talking to the other guard.

"Well, well." Sergei stopped short when he saw me. "Aren't you a sight for sore eyes," he said with a pleased smile.

I smiled too, rising, not sure if I was supposed to stay seated or what.

"Kat," he said, coming around the table to give me a hug while the guards stood back and let us. "I'm glad you came."

He looked good, remarkably so. He wore a uniform in the same shade of beige as the walls, but I guess I'd expected him to look thinner or older or something.

"What is it?" he asked me after our hug.

"Oh, I just thought," I stammered, feeling embarrassed. "I thought you'd look different I guess." I sounded so stupid.

"I'm lucky. My boys take good care of me," he said, gesturing to the guards.

His *boys*?

Wow. We both sat down.

"How are you, Kat? I hope that son of mine is treating you all right?"

"I'm okay. Club is doing well. It's always busy, you know."

"I know. And Alexi?"

I glanced at my lap for a minute then told myself I had to do this. I needed to. "That's why I'm here, actually."

He didn't look surprised. "Go on."

"I appreciate everything you did for me and realize now maybe I shouldn't have been so eager to accept—"

"Accept what?"

"The advance. The apartment."

"It was a trade. I needed you to play piano, and I needed you to look good doing it. You made me money, Kat. It was a business transaction."

"Alexi thinks I owe that money to the club. He's been taking it out of my checks, and…" I shook my head and looked away. "I wouldn't have come, but I'm…he wants things, Sergei, and I can't—"

Sergei's eyes hardened, and he raised his hand to his chin, rubbing the stubble there, studying me.

"My son is overstepping. As usual."

"I'm sorry, I'm sure this isn't a great time for me to come to you with this. I just didn't know what else to do."

"Does he want you to work one of the parties?"

"You know about those?"

Sergei's lips curved upward. "I always appreciated your naiveté."

More like my stupidity.

He sat back in his chair and cocked his head to the side. "Tell him yes," he said out of the blue.

"What?"

"Agree to work the party."

"But—"

"I'll double whatever he pays you and make sure any debt is wiped out."

"I—"

"You'll do a little business for me and take care of the problem of my son at once."

"What business?"

He leaned in close, smiled a little, and gave me a wink. "Come now, let's be straight with each other. It's not as though you came to me without your own agenda, is it? *Lina?*"

My mouth fell open, and I found it suddenly hard to breathe. Did he know who I was all along? Was I so stupid?

"I've always been curious what it was you were looking for, honestly. Your grandfather and I... Well, we were friends once."

He watched me, letting the awkward pause hang in the air between us.

"There's nothing to tie me to your grandfather now, is there? If there were, I'm sure it would be very bad for him...for you, and well, everyone...so let's get on the same page about that. There's nothing to that, is there?"

"You knew who I was all along."

He sat back in his chair, ignoring my comment. "Is there?"

I shook my head slowly, feeling color drain from my skin at my lie.

"Good. Then we can move on. A server, Kat. Nothing more."

"But..."

"I want to know about a few possible attendees.

I'll have my attorney forward the particular names and faces I'm looking for."

"I don't understand, Sergei."

"Nothing to understand. I need something, and you need something. This is a business transaction. Do this for me, and I'll make sure to get Alexi off your back. In fact, you'll be free of any ties to my family at all. I guarantee it."

"Mr. Markov," one of the guards said.

"Just a minute."

Sergei kept his eyes on me, soft as stone.

"Think about it. You'll be free. You'll have to leave town, of course. Alexi never did like for me to take away his toys."

He stood.

I watched him tower over me. I'd thought he was like a father to me. Had I been so desperate for parental affection that I'd clung to the tiniest bit of it? Because Sergei—this Sergei—wasn't the man I remembered.

"Thanks for coming in to see me." He spoke casually again, a smile not quite warming his face. "I'd much rather look at your pretty face than at these two," he said about the guards.

They all chuckled, and Sergei leaned in to hug me. I realized why when I felt his hot breath at my ear.

"The apartment is bugged," he whispered.

"Stanley will arrange everything. Just let him know on your way back."

When he pulled away, and I opened my mouth to speak, he set his finger over his lips to tell me to be quiet.

"Thanks for coming, Kat."

I watched the guards lead him out. The door behind me opened, and the one who'd escorted me in now escorted me out where Stanley waited patiently for me. Even him I saw in a different light now. They were all involved in this strange and dangerous game.

The expression keep your friends close and your enemies closer never made more sense than this moment.

13

LINA

When Stanley pulled up to the apartment, I immediately saw Alexi's SUV parked out front. My heart thudded as we neared, and I met Stanley's eyes in the rearview mirror.

"Shall I keep driving?" he asked as he slowed.

The SUV's driver's side door opened, and Maxx climbed out, his eyes locking on mine through the front windshield. He leaned against the car and folded his arms. Alexi wasn't with him. But that didn't mean anything.

"No, Stanley, this is fine." I had to face the music sometime.

"All right." He turned to me, waiting for something.

I cleared my throat. "Sergei said you'd arrange

things?" He smiled and handed me a card from inside his pocket.

"Call this number. Let him know who you are. And if you need me again, just call the service. They'll get a hold of me."

He was still smiling, but I saw that smile differently than I used to. Any warmth seemed to have leeched out of it.

"Thank you," I said, taking the card.

"My pleasure."

I climbed out of the car and grabbed my bag. Bypassing the stairs to the apartment, I went directly to the SUV, where Maxx opened the back door and waited for me to climb in before closing it. He gave me a wary look in the rearview mirror, started the car, and drove toward the club. Neither of us spoke the entire way, and I didn't bother to check my phone for a message from Damon. I knew there would be one by now, and to hear his voice would test my resolve.

We arrived at Club Carmen before opening, so we only passed a handful of staff on our way to Alexi's office. Maxx walked me to it, staying close behind me as if I might try to run. As if I could get away from them. All the while, my meeting with Sergei played in my mind. What he wanted. The alternative to having to be Alexi's whore.

When we got to the office, Maxx reached over my head to knock on the door before opening it.

Alexi sat behind his desk. When he saw me, he leaned back in his seat, his face hard and cold.

"Well, well, well, the prodigal server."

"Um, I don't think you're using that word correctly." Not my smartest move, but I couldn't help it.

He stood and walked around his desk. I heard the door close and saw Maxx take up his position beside it, his big arms folded, watching but invisible.

"I'd shut your mouth if I were you," Alexi said.

He perched on the edge of his desk and cocked his head to the side as he looked at me.

"Take off your coat."

I did, folding it over the back of the chair he didn't invite me to sit on.

"Don't you look...refreshed? Sunny even. Certainly not getting that color here in freezing Manhattan, are you?"

"Something came up. I had to go out of town."

"That so?"

"Yes."

"What exactly came up?"

"A friend needed me in Florida. I went to help her."

"Her?"

"Yes."

He came toward me, arms at his sides. I remembered how he'd slapped me once and instinctively prepared for him to do it again. He must have liked that because he chuckled.

"Who was she with, Maxx?" Alexi asked, eyes on me.

"Stepping out of a taxi on her own, sir."

What?

I glanced quickly over at Maxx, who looked straight ahead, then back at Alexi.

Why had he just lied? If he'd told Alexi I'd climbed out of a private car with a driver, Alexi would have known it was his father's. But why would Maxx lie to protect me?

Was it to protect me?

Alexi's cold, pale eyes bore into mine before he circled me, standing so close I felt his breath on my shoulder.

He inhaled.

"I don't smell sex on you, but that only means you weren't recently fucked."

"What business is it of yours if I was?"

"Were you?"

"What do you want, Alexi?"

"I want to know why you walked out when you were supposed to be working the party. You left the other servers to pick up your slack. And I want to know how in hell you disappeared to Florida for two days given your financial situation, not to mention calling in sick at the last minute and leaving me in the lurch."

"Look, I'm sorry about that, but it was unavoidable that I go. This was a good friend who got into an accident and needed me. I couldn't leave her stranded. She paid for my ticket. As for leaving the party," I paused, dropping my head. Alexi still stood behind me, hovering like the freaking Grim Reaper. I turned to face him. "Honestly, Alexi, I got scared," I said, trying to look pitiful. "And I know it was wrong to leave like that, but all those people and the things that were going on—"

He held up a hand to stop me and turned to Maxx. "You can step outside."

Maxx nodded and left the room.

"Go on."

"I was going to ask you if I could make up the time, actually. I felt bad for leaving, and I'm ready for it now. Now that I know what to expect. And as you know, I could use the money. If that's okay with you, of course."

He studied my face, obviously having trouble believing me.

"What the fuck is going on, Kat?"

"What do you mean?"

"Your sudden interest in attending a party?"

"I make more money, which means I can pay you back faster and get on with my life."

He didn't look convinced.

"You owe me for leaving early. It fucked with the night."

"I'm sorry. I just...it was too much, Alexi. Really."

"There's a party on Wednesday night," he said.

"There is?" Shit. I knew I had to do it, but every instinct told me no. Told me to run.

"If you're serious about this—"

"I am. I just...it's hard, you can understand?"

"Midnight Wednesday. I'll see you upstairs. If you're not there—"

"I'll be there. I promise."

He resumed his seat behind his desk and picked up a pen. I remained standing, waiting for him to dismiss me. He liked doing that.

"You're excused."

Fuck you. "Thanks."

With that, I left, declining Maxx's offer to drive me home and choosing to walk instead. I took out my phone and the card Stanley had given me. The secretary put me through right away, and when I said my name, he knew exactly who I was and told me he'd have a folder couriered to the apartment. I thanked him and hung up then braced myself to listen to the voice mail messages.

Damon had left three. The first must have been before he'd gotten back to the hotel because it was playful. It twisted my heart to hear it. The next wasn't playful. Not at all. And the final one, well, I listened to it as I turned the corner to the brownstone, not at all surprised to find him waiting there for me.

He gave me a hard look, and I didn't smile. Instead, I retrieved my key and unlocked the door, letting him follow me inside.

14

DAMON

"This is getting old," Lina said as she slid her arms out of her coat and turned to me.

"It's so far past old, you have no fucking idea."

I fumed. I'd been worrying since the moment I got back to the hotel to find our room empty, all her things gone. No note. Nothing. But the moment she'd turned the corner, that worry had turned to white-hot anger.

Taking her by the arm, I dragged her into the bedroom.

"What are you doing?" She resisted but wasn't much of a match physically.

"I'm taking you up on your earlier offer."

"What?"

I slammed the bedroom door shut behind us and

tossed her onto the bed, inadvertently tearing her blouse a little when I did.

"Stop!"

She scrambled away, but I caught her by the waistband of her jeans and yanked her back.

"Take them off." Holding her to me, I undid them for her, her effort to free herself laughable as I tugged her jeans and panties down to her knees, not giving her a chance to do it herself. I spun her around and pushed her to bend over the edge of the bed, pressing one knee into her back to keep her there as I unbuckled my belt.

"Damon!"

She struggled beneath me, craning her neck to look back, to watch me double the belt over and grip the buckle in my hand.

I met her gaze, fury making my breath short and tight as I forced myself to count to ten before I began.

"You fucked up, Lina."

"Damon, I know. I just…I—"

"I told you we'd work through this together." I raised my arm. She fisted the bedcovers, readying herself. I swung, the sound of leather on flesh jarring.

Lina cried out.

I struck again.

"These are dangerous men."

Two wicked red welts appeared on her ass.

"I told you I'd be back. I told you I wouldn't leave you to handle this alone." Three more crisscrossed those.

"Damon, listen to me—" She let out another cry at the next stroke.

"No. I'm done listening. It's your turn now. And I'm going to let my belt do the talking."

For the next five minutes, the only sounds in the room were those of leather lashing flesh, Lina's cries, and my tight breathing. Throughout her punishment, she never once said she was sorry. And I didn't think she was. Not about leaving like she had.

When she stopped struggling and lay prone, I moved my knee off her back and looked at her, bent over the edge of the bed, her jeans down around her ankles, her blouse halfway up her back, her bare ass and thighs striped red.

She buried her face in the bed, handfuls of the comforter fisted in her hands, and waited for more.

"You didn't even leave a fucking note." My voice was quieter, and I felt calmer than I had when I'd arrived, when I'd first seen her.

She twisted backward to look at me. "Punish me, Damon. I deserve it."

I realized that at some point during her punishment, my cock had hardened. I thought how wrong it was that it should be, now, at this, at my hurting her.

"You're right. You do. Stretch your arms to either side of the bed."

She did so slowly.

"Get up on the tips of your toes and arch your back. I want your ass out."

She pulled her legs straighter, stood high on tiptoe, her ass offered to me.

"Don't move a muscle."

I raised my arm and struck again. Her breath caught on a squeak and she rounded her back but only for an instant before resuming her position for more. I could glimpse her pussy between her cheeks. I wanted to whip that too.

A sound came from deep inside me, and I lashed her again, harder than before, wanting to punish her for this, for my desire, for making me want her. For fucking making me want her like this.

"Open your legs."

She widened her stance so I could see all of her now. She lay her cheek on the bed and slid one hand between her thighs. I could see her fingers working. I could hear it.

I raised my arm and lashed her again.

She cried out, closing her eyes, arching her back for more while she fingered her cunt. My dick raged against my jeans. It wanted her.

"God. Why do you do this to me?" I asked not sure who I was asking as I struck again.

She let out a grunt, a mewl, and reached her other arm back to open her pussy lips.

"Fuck me. Please fuck me."

"I'm not done whipping you," I said. "Stretch your arms out. You don't get to come on my belt."

She obeyed, a supplicant.

And I punished her while my guilt punished me.

Her skin turned a fiery red. I tightened the grip on my belt.

Who was I? Who the fuck was I?

Her eyes burned when I met them. I threw the belt on the floor, the buckle making a loud clanging sound when it hit the hardwood. I put my hands on her ass my throat working to swallow as I drew her apart and looked at her. Her flesh burned the palms of my hands. I rubbed two fingers over her wet pussy that dripped onto her thighs.

I met her gaze and held it.

She didn't move but bit her lip.

"God, Lina. I don't want to want you."

"I need you, Damon," she whispered. "I need you inside me."

"This is wrong," I said, shaking my head because as much as I knew how wrong it was, as much as I knew the sin I committed, I knew what I would do. I couldn't resist this temptation.

"Please. I need this. I need you."

I shifted my gaze to her ass, unzipped my jeans and

shoved them down to mid-thigh. Fisting my cock, I guided myself into her pussy, closing my eyes as I slid into her, warmth engulfing me, a sense of homecoming.

"Why do you put her on my path?" I asked my God while I fucked her. How fucked up was this? How fucked up was I?

"Make me come, Damon. I need to come."

I fucked her hard, moving deep inside her swearing this would be it. I'd stop after this. I'd stop. I'd give her what she needed. Take what I needed just once more, and then I'd stop.

"I need you so much," she whimpered.

I looked at her.

Just this one time. Just this one more time, then I'd let her go. Then I'd do the right thing.

I needed this too. I needed to be close to her. She squeezed her eyes shut, her hands clenching around the sheets.

"Why did you leave like that?" I asked, not expecting—not even wanting—an answer. My eyes were riveted on her ass, on my cock disappearing inside her pussy. Inside her wet, pink cunt.

"Damon."

She reached back with one hand and took hold of mine, clutching it tightly as I lay myself over her, sweat dripping from my forehead onto her face, my chest to her back, still thrusting, not wanting an inch of space between us, needing to hold her, as if being inside her wasn't close enough. Like I could never be close enough.

"You make me do things, Lina—"

"Come inside me. I want to feel you. All of you."

Fuck. Fuck. Fuck.

I held her hand and gripped her hair with the other, twisting her head so I could kiss her face, the side of her mouth.

Resisting her was too hard. Too fucking hard. I felt like some animal, like a beast, a wild, rutting beast. And I couldn't stop. I couldn't get close enough, and when her breath hitched and her pussy throbbed around my cock and she made a desperate sound, I stilled inside her and came.

Fuck, I came hard.

I emptied into her, heaven and hell waging their twisted war inside me as I gave myself over to ecstasy, knowing it was fleeting, knowing this was all I could give. All I could have.

Knowing this would be the last time.

Knowing it had to be.

And as the orgasm faded, a bitterness settled heavily in my gut.

I straightened and pulled out. I watched as my seed spilled out of her, slid down her thighs. It was all I could do. Because I couldn't look at her, not at her eyes. Not yet.

She stood. The torn blouse she still wore fell to the tops of her thighs to cover her, to shield her from my sight. I pulled on my jeans, picked up my belt, and wound it through the loops before finally facing her, almost looking at her.

Lina touched a hand to her matted, wild hair, looking disoriented.

I rubbed my face, the stubble on my jaw. "Get dressed."

"What?"

I was at the door. I paused and almost turned around. "I didn't come here for this. I didn't come here to do *this*." I slammed my fist against the door frame and heard her gasp behind me. "Damnit! God, I didn't come here for *this*!" Was I speaking to him? Angry with *him*? For *my* weakness?

"I hate your God," came Lina's small whisper.

I turned to face her. Saw the tears brimming in her eyes, saw how her lips had narrowed, how she clenched handfuls of her own wild hair.

"I hate him. I fucking hate him."

I had done this to her. "Lina—"

"Get out."

I rubbed my face, wrapped my hands around the back of my neck.

"Go. Get out, Damon. Get the hell out. Out of my apartment." She came at me, pounding her fists into my chest. "Out of my life."

I grabbed hold of her wrists and looked into her sad, mossy-green eyes that were shiny and bright with tears. She knew this was it. She knew this was the last time.

"Go." Her voice broke, and she dropped her head, stepping back.

I let her go and watched as she slumped on the edge of the bed where I'd just fucked her. In the room that smelled of us, of sex and sweat, the comforter half on the bed, half off. Lina slid down to sit on the floor, her face in her hands.

Maybe this was for the best.

Fuck.

How could it be for the best? How could I leave her like this? No God would want me to leave her like this. Not even the one she hated. The same one I'd chosen.

Chosen over her.

Fuck.

"I love you," I said, the words catching in my throat, making me feel as though I'd choke. "But this is a mistake." I leaned against the wall and slid down to my haunches as her eyes met mine. My heart thudded against my chest, and blood pumped inside my ears, making it hard to think. Making it fucking impossible. It took all I had to keep looking at her, to see the damage I'd done, the damage I was doing. The hurt I'd caused out of my own selfishness. My need. My desire. "I'm so sorry."

"Get out."

This time, she said it so quietly, I wasn't sure she'd spoken at all.

"Get out, Damon." Her voice cracked.

I stumbled, then stood. "I'm going to help you." I said as I went to her and tried to lift her to stand.

Lina shoved my hands away and stood on her own. I saw the effort it took for her to do so. To keep upright.

"You don't hear me," she said. "You don't want to hear me."

"Lina—"

"I'm calling the police if you don't get out now," she said, picking up the receiver. "I'll tell them you broke in here. That you raped me."

I opened my mouth to speak, taken aback by her words.

"I guess the church wouldn't want you then, would they?" she asked, her back straighter, her voice full of venom.

I went to her, wrapped my hands around her arms, and sat her down on the bed. She let me this time, let me touch her as easily as she let the phone slip from her hand as her face fell.

She dropped her forehead to my chest. "I'm tired. I am so tired. Please just go. Let me sleep."

She wouldn't look at me but I felt her tears on my shirt.

"I'm going to get you out of this mess with Alexi," I said.

She didn't reply.

"I'm going to fix this. Get you your life back."

She shook her head and finally raised her gaze to mine. "A life without you in it."

"You know it can't happen."

She smiled but tears poured down her cheeks. "Get out. Go to your church. Your God. No. Better yet. Go to hell, Damon."

15

LINA

I slept all that day and the next, waking up the following night with a gnawing hunger in my belly even though the thought of food made me nauseous. I wasn't sure if I expected the hurt to be any less, but it wasn't. Was it worse because he told me he loved me? Had he meant to even say it?

I climbed into the shower to scrub myself, to scrub away the last of his touch, his scent. I wept as I washed, wept the loss of him. I'd known I'd lose him, though. I'd known it all along.

I just didn't know it would hurt this badly.

After getting dressed, I made myself a cup of coffee and downed Advil with a swallow of it. My head throbbed, and my heart hurt. Every time I sat, my bruised, punished flesh reminded me of him, of what he'd done. Of what we'd done.

I stood in my apartment—no, not mine. Sergei's.

Alexi's. I remembered what Sergei had told me, that it was bugged. If that were true, they'd have a field day with what they'd heard. But why would it be bugged? For me? It couldn't be for Sergei. I got the impression he'd never lived here. Maybe it was for Alexi?

But all that paled in comparison as Damon's words repeated in my head. The look on his face when he'd said them. When he'd told me he loved me.

Although it didn't matter, did it? He didn't love me enough to stay. He didn't love me enough to choose me.

I set my coffee mug down, tears coming anew. I went into the bedroom, where the scent of us hit me like a tsunami. Like a mad woman, I tore the comforter off, then the sheets. That was when Damon's wallet rolled onto the floor.

I looked at it, surprised. It must have fallen out of his pocket.

Sitting on the stripped bed, I held it, held it like one held onto hope. Even though I knew I shouldn't. That nothing would change. It couldn't. He'd already chosen, and he hadn't chosen me.

Setting the wallet down, I lay in the unmade bed and pulled the bare comforter over me. Tomorrow, I'd return the wallet to him. Tomorrow, I'd give back the last piece of him that I still held. Because I didn't want to keep any part of him. I couldn't. It hurt too much.

WHEN I WOKE in the morning, I got dressed and was ready to leave when I noticed the large envelope someone had slipped beneath the door. My heart beat fast as I stooped to pick it up, knowing what it was. I opened it to find one large folder and a smaller envelope inside. I took out the smaller one and opened the flap.

"Shit."

A stack of bills greeted me, new, crisp, and green. All hundreds.

No. Not again. There had to be five thousand dollars in here. I'd told Sergei no. I looked for a note of explanation, but there wasn't one. Really, didn't the cash explain itself? I was in the employ of a Russian mobster. A currently jailed Russian mobster.

Setting that aside, I opened the larger envelope and spread the photos out on the coffee table. There were five eight by ten photographs, four men and one woman. I recognized two of the men, and if I wasn't sure before, the warnings bells sounding in my head told me now that this was a bad idea.

Of the two I recognized, one was a regular at Club Carmen or had been for a while but had recently stopped coming altogether. The other, the one that baffled me more, was the photograph of Maxx, Alexi's trusted bodyguard.

What the hell was this? Why did Sergei care about either of them? What was he up to?

The other three varied in age from about thirty to fifty, the woman being the oldest. Two were Russian, one Asian. Their names, ages, and distinguishing marks were written on the back. I wondered if he listed those because the party guests typically wore masks.

I studied the images, trying to memorize the details, and decided I wouldn't take the money. I'd return it to Stanley.

But then what?

What would I do after it was done? Go back to Italy? Live with Sofia and Raphael, be reminded of Damon every time I looked at Raphael because they were as identical as could be, physically at least? No. That door had closed to me. At least for now. I'd need to leave New York, though. Sergei had told me that much.

Packing up the photos, I went into the bedroom and hid them between the mattress and box spring. There was no telling when Alexi would drop by, and I knew Sergei wouldn't want him finding those.

That brought me to Maxx. Did him lying to Alexi have anything to do with the fact that he was in the stack of photos Sergei sent? Alexi must have known

Stanley worked for Sergei Markov. Alexi would have wanted to know what the hell I was doing with him if he found out, and I thought Maxx was loyal to Alexi. Was he?

Shaking my head, I grabbed my coat and purse. I dropped Damon's wallet inside it. I needed to get this done.

Rather than taking a cab, I walked the half hour to the church, hoping to collect my courage. The sky was clear, although the weather reports warned of another storm coming in. My heart raced as I turned the corner. I'd already decided I would leave it in a pew for him to find rather than knocking on his door. I couldn't chance seeing him again. I just wasn't strong enough.

Once I got to the church, I glanced down the alley that led to his door. It was empty. I went around to the church's front entrance and pulled the large door open. The familiar scent of incense and candles engulfed me. All that prayer, hope, and despair hung heavy in the air.

I walked in. I was alone. Mass would have ended half an hour ago. Would I run into him here? Would he be wearing his cassock? What would he do, what would he think, to see me here?

And what would I do if I saw him like that? Even though I didn't know Damon as part of the church, he was.

I took a few steps into the softly lit space. Hardly

any sunlight penetrated the intricately drawn stained glass of the windows. Sconces along the walls were dimmed but left on for those who would wander in to pray. The church doors remained unlocked during the day.

I looked up toward the altar. Soft red glowed: the tabernacle lamp. A constantly burning beacon—except on Good Friday. The day of Christ's execution. Why did I remember that?

A chill ran along my spine.

I walked up the center aisle, even the quiet rubber soles of my boots sounding too loud here, in this still, silent place. Maybe it was because I wanted to remain invisible, even from the long dead icons that decorated the walls.

The crucifix that hung over the altar seemed to grow larger as I neared, and even though Christ's eyes were closed, I felt those of the others on me. The saints. The martyrs.

I'd been raised Catholic, but it had never meant much to me. I'd never felt anything one way or another. I didn't puzzle away at philosophical questions, didn't wonder if God existed. I didn't care. Why did I tremble now? Why did my breath come short and strangled and sweat bead across my forehead? What was it I felt? Not the nothing I expected to feel.

Looking at Jesus hanging on the cross now, there,

before me, large as life—larger than *my* life—felt strange. Wrong.

I felt wrong.

I felt jealous.

Silence, like a tangible thing, stood still here, surrounding me. I stopped at the top of the aisle, steps from the altar, and just looked up at it.

At him.

As though he held some part of Damon, some piece of him I did not. A piece I never would.

But I also felt a guilty triumph. Because I'd taken something he never could.

I'd had Damon inside me.

I'd taken his seed inside me.

Shouldn't that make him mine? At least in some small way?

Couldn't that be enough?

A side door opened, and my heart leaped into my throat. I turned just as he stopped, both of us seeing each other at the same instant. Damon stood at the side door, framed by elaborate wood molding, wearing black from head to toe. But not the cassock. At least it wasn't the cassock.

He cleared his throat and entered, closing the door behind him. The sound of his shoes on the stone floor reverberated off the walls as he approached me. He, too, like Christ on his cross, grew larger as he neared, made me tilt my head back to see him.

I don't think I breathed a single breath as my heart pounded against my chest.

Damon's blue eyes searched my face, his gaze moved over my body, my coat buttoned up tight to my neck. His gaze fell to my hand, and a moment later, his closed around it.

I looked down to where he held me.

No.

Held *it*. The wallet.

I'd forgotten.

He was taking his wallet. That was all. He wasn't holding me.

But he didn't move, and he didn't speak. He just kept my hand wrapped up inside his. When I turned my face back to his and opened my mouth to tell him I'd come to bring it to him, I couldn't.

I picked up the faint scent of aftershave beneath the incense filling the space. It was like this small part of him, of Damon, separate of this place, of the church, of Jesus. Of God. Damon as man. Damon, human. Damon, flesh and blood and human.

Corruptible.

Corrupt.

No.

I broke our gaze and shook my head.

That was me. I was the corrupt one.

What was I doing? What was I thinking? Why had I come here truly?

I stepped back and drew my hand free of his.

The wallet fell to the floor with a soft thud, sounding much louder to me than it could sound in reality.

"Lina..."

This was wrong. What I was doing here, why I'd come, why I'd truly come...what I wanted...wanting him when he didn't belong to me. Couldn't belong to me because he had promised himself to another.

I glanced at the crucifix again, and I swear I felt the accusation, the condemnation, the wrath coming from the closed eyes of the dead Christ.

I was a thief. I would steal Damon away.

I looked at Damon again, his blue eyes steady on me, watching me, filled with something that made them appear darker...filled with sadness.

Or perhaps that was regret. Regret over what we'd done.

Without my consent, my fingers reached up to touch his face, skin soft and warm. Freshly shaved. Not rough like it had been when I'd last seen him.

His hand wrapped around my wrist, not pulling mine away, but not drawing me to him either. His thumb rubbed against my palm, and I found myself stepping closer, unable to resist him.

"What are you doing?" he whispered, his voice raw.

The door opened just then, and Damon stepped away, releasing me. I glanced at the man who stood in the doorway. Another priest. I looked down at my feet.

The older man cleared his throat.

I didn't even look back up. Didn't look at Damon one last time. Instead, feeling a deep shame, I turned and walked quickly out of the church, something hot growing inside my belly, rising to my chest, something that would fill my throat in another moment, a thing that would shatter me if I didn't let it out, if I didn't let it rage.

"I'm sorry," I said to no one as I pushed the heavy doors open and stepped out onto the street where the early morning sun had given way to dark clouds.

Wind foretold of the storm to come. A gust lifted my hair off my shoulders and had me hugging my arms around myself as I ran away from the church, ran from Damon, from God. My vision blurred as I willed myself to disappear from here, willed the earth to open up and swallow me whole and obliterate my mind, obliterate me, so I wouldn't have to think, to feel, not anymore. Not about him. Not about Sofia or Alexi or Sergei. Not about what I had to do.

Not about the feeling deep inside my gut that told me I was going to lose everything. That I hadn't come close yet to the loss I was due.

Because I still hadn't paid the price for my sin.

For trying to steal Damon away from his God. I still owed, and I'd still be made to pay.

16

DAMON

I didn't care that Father Leonard stood watching me. That he'd seen us. Seen how close we'd stood. Had he felt the tension in the air that seemed to unravel any peace, anything holy here, that blasphemed against the sacredness of this most sacred place.

All I could do was watch the space where she'd been, look at the closed doors from which she'd exited. It was like she was a ghost. Like she hadn't been there at all. That's how fleeting it had been. An instant. A moment in time.

"Damon," Father Leonard's said in a deep tenor.

I didn't turn. I didn't care. Tightness swelled in my gut, sealed my throat. As I bent to pick up the wallet she'd returned, I closed my eyes and breathed in deeply, willing the breaking to stop, to wait at least until I was alone. Until I *could* break. Until there was no one to bear witness.

But when Father Leonard's hand touched my shoulder, I fell to my knees and dropped my head in shame—shame at my weakness—and agony, the loss of her like a weight in my gut, like a rope around my neck.

He didn't speak, and neither did I. A few minutes later, he squeezed my shoulder and quietly left. Left me there on the floor, on my knees before the altar. I looked up at it. At the crucified Christ. At the candles burning before him. At the Tabernacle lamp.

Body and blood of Christ.

What was it we made of it? What was this thing, this ceremony to celebrate the most holy? What did we seek? Salvation? Absolution? Comfort? Love? Wasn't that what it was all about?

Church was where this had begun. Where the seed of doubt germinated. Four years ago in Pienza. Four years ago when her sister had been with my brother. Lina had been waiting for Sofia to come and, when she hadn't, I'd stepped in.

It was just an outing, me showing her one of my favorite Tuscan villages. After lunch, we'd gone into the church there. A beautiful, ancient structure. It had been empty of tourists, which was strange that time of year.

Lina had been sixteen. I'd been twenty-four. Fucking twenty-four. But it had been innocent.

We'd sat in the cool, quiet place, the second to last pew from the back. I'd said a prayer. I still remember the moment I realized I'd been saying it aloud. I found her watching me, her face intent, eyes wide.

"I've never seen someone so...lost...in prayer," she'd said. "You're truly devoted."

"I'm not. I have more doubts than you can imagine."

I stared at her, taken aback myself at my admission.

She gave me a faint smile and slipped her hand beneath mine on the church pew. Not over it, but underneath.

A strange sensation had bubbled in my gut, something brand-new. Something filling me with...hope.

I still remembered how Lina had watched me. And for all the faith in the world, I couldn't pull my hand away, couldn't drag my gaze away. I shifted my hand a little so my fingers wound around hers.

There was something in that touch, in that gaze, that shouldn't have been there.

That *I* shouldn't have allowed.

To this day, I don't know why I did that. To this day, I never confessed it. Not to a single soul.

But I repented. Because it ruined her. Because then, like now, she was vulnerable and young, and I was selfish. I didn't even have the excuse of youth anymore. Celibacy perhaps. A lack of that sort of...entertainment.

Whatever it was, I'd known then it was wrong,

and I knew now it was wrong. But the reasons were different.

Then, it was wrong because I was committed to the church, to Christ. To God.

Now, it was wrong because I was of two minds. And I dragged her along without any thought of her. Of how she would hurt. Of how I'd hurt her. Damage her. Ruin her. This time, permanently.

17

LINA

The night of the party, I had an early shift at the club. Once it was over, I'd head upstairs to the penthouse to change, wondering what ridiculous outfit he'd have me in this time. If I'd be painted gold again. I hated that paint. It made me feel like I couldn't breathe. But if things went as planned, tonight would be it. I'd be done.

Except that when I got upstairs, Maxx was waiting for me just off the elevator.

"Kat," he said, gesturing down the hallway with a cocking of his head.

"I'm supposed to be serving. I think this is the changing room," I said, pointing to the door straight ahead, which opened as I finished my sentence, and two girls stepped into the hallway. This time, they were painted silver instead of gold, and instead of the thong we were allowed the other time, they each wore a fine silver chain that hung from their hips and hooked onto a ring each girl had pierced on her lower lips.

I admit, I stared, shocked, until Maxx cleared his throat.

"This way. Mr. Markov is waiting for you."

I allowed myself to be led toward a door I'd never entered before. He opened it and stood aside. As far as the eye could see, everything was either red or gold—carpets, curtains, the upholstery on the furnishings. It all reeked of too much money and too little taste.

He led me through the main room to another one, where Alexi sat behind a desk, reading something on a laptop. When we walked in, he closed the lid of the laptop and looked up at me. Maxx stood back at the door, folding his arms across his chest.

"Kat." Not quite a greeting. "Sit."

I obeyed.

"You look...tired."

"I'm fine. Just anxious about the party."

"Hmm." He stood and walked around the desk to lean against it. He folded his arms across his chest and cocked his head to the side. "Anxious, huh?"

"I guess."

He shifted his gaze to the ceiling, then back to me. Every movement seemed calculated, purposeful. It made me nervous.

"Trust is a difficult thing to earn, hmm?"

"I suppose so."

"It's important to trust one's employees, isn't it? For example, Maxx. I trust him. He and I go way back, isn't that right, Maxx?"

Silence as Maxx stood at the door, unresponsive and looking at something just beyond me. I guess he knew he wasn't meant to respond.

"When they put my father behind bars, I had to challenge each of his employees. I had to start from scratch. I let many go. But I still made mistakes."

I shifted in my seat, imagining what he meant by *letting many go*.

"You know my father and I don't exactly see eye to eye. Never really have."

"I'm not sure what this has to do with me, Alexi."

He stretched his arms out and studied his fingernails. "Your relationship with my father was a close one, wasn't it?"

"I don't know what you're getting at."

"I know you don't like to let on that he fucked you, and I understand that. People would lose respect."

"I didn't. He didn't."

"I mean, I ignore the rumors. I understand what jealousy can be like, especially for such an attractive young woman."

"Get to the point, Alexi."

He gripped the lip of the desk, still facing me. "Did you talk to my father that way?"

"There was nothing between us. And even if there was, why do you care?"

"How is dad?" His question came abruptly. Unexpectedly.

"What?" My mouth was a desert.

"How is he? I admit, I haven't been to see him. What did dear old dad want? You know, when you visited him the other day."

My heart raced. He knew. Shit. He knew. I glanced at Maxx, who stood still, studying the far wall, blocking the exit. Not that I could get away, not if Alexi didn't want me to.

"I was close to him," I said after clearing my throat. "Like you said. I wanted to visit him. See how he was holding up."

One side of Alexi's lips curved upward. "You don't think me stupid, do you?"

"Alexi..." I felt out of control, powerless. This wasn't how tonight was supposed to go. "Of course not."

Alexi lifted the receiver off his desk and told whoever was on the line "there's one more." A moment later, the door behind his desk opened, and an older, ragged woman appeared. She stood there and gave me a once-over, her mouth a thin line. She looked either bored or annoyed.

"Stand up, Kat."

Maxx took a step forward.

"Alexi—" I started.

"Up. Party will begin soon. I need you in makeup. You won't bring me much, looking like that, will you? Now get up."

"No," I said, shaking my head, clutching my bag tightly when Maxx crossed the room. His hands fell to either of my arms, lifting me to my feet. "I didn't agree to this."

"What you agreed or didn't agree to doesn't matter anymore. You forfeited any rights when you decided to go against me."

"But, Alexi!" Maxx began to walk me to the door, to where the woman stood aside, unfazed. "Please!"

Alexi opened a drawer and withdrew something familiar: the folder I'd hidden between the mattress and box spring of my bed. But when he opened it and set the photos out, I noticed there were only four of them. The one of Maxx was missing.

"Get her out of my sight."

Alexi resumed his seat behind his desk. Maxx led me through the door and down the hallway to another room. There, he held me tight as the woman cut through my clothes with a pair of scissors and stripped everything from me, even snipping my bra and panties before laying me on a cold metal table and binding my wrists and ankles to it, even strapping a leather restraint across my forehead so I couldn't move my head.

"Is she a screamer? You know I hate the noise," the woman said to Maxx.

"She won't be a screamer," Maxx said, meeting my gaze. "Will you?"

I took one look at his huge arms and hands, not wanting to know the damage they could do. I muttered a 'no' as the woman began to prepare me for what I knew would be the auction. I berated myself for my stupidity, for my naiveté. For letting myself be put in this position.

I'd be beaten tonight. And raped. Or worse. I didn't know. All I knew was that I'd given up my freedom the moment I'd gone to Sergei for help.

18

DAMON

Father Leonard hadn't exactly accused me of anything, but he'd seen Lina and me together. He'd seen how we'd looked at each other. He wasn't a stupid man. He'd only mentioned in passing that if I wanted to talk, his door was always open.

I wondered if he knew Gavin had sent me here. The real reason why I'd been banished from seminary.

I checked my phone on my way up the stairs to my apartment, still holding onto hope that she would call, but there were no messages. I slid the phone into my pocket and dug out my keys to the apartment, but when I got to it, I found the door slightly ajar. A dim light came from inside.

Cautious, I pushed it open and stopped. There, on the couch at the far end of the room, sat Alexi

Markov. He had one leg crossed over the other and was flipping through a magazine. He closed it when he saw me and gave me what I imagined was supposed to be a smile.

I stepped into the room, and as soon as I did, the door closed behind me. I turned to find a second man standing in front of it as if he expected me to turn and run.

I had no intention of running. In fact, the bastard had saved me a trip.

"Where's Lina?" I asked, imagining her alone with these men. How vulnerable she'd be in every way. I was a man. If nothing else, I could fight.

Alexi cocked his head to the side, raising his eyebrows slightly, then turned his attention to picking a cuticle, which he tossed onto the floor.

"So, this is the man." He ignored my question. "The one who's got my girl running off to fucking Florida at the drop of a hat." His gaze ran over me. "A priest, no less."

I stepped toward him, but the man behind me closed his hand over my shoulder, halting me.

"I hope you don't mind us dropping by like this," Alexi continued.

"Where's Lina?"

Alexi uncrossed his legs and leaned forward, glancing around. "Who?"

"You know who. Where is she?" Fuck. If he'd hurt her, I'd never forgive myself. How could I have left her alone in that apartment, knowing he came and went as he pleased? Suspecting this was all out of her control. I should never have left this up to her. I should have dragged her kicking and screaming back to Tuscany.

He grinned and leaned over to lift a magazine off the coffee table. "Is she under here, perhaps? She's little, isn't she?" he added, peeking under a paperweight next.

"If you've hurt her—"

"Me? Hurt *Lina*? No. Kat, as I know her, is fine. Splendid, in fact. I wouldn't hurt a hair on her pretty head."

For some reason, I believed him. He was here to warn me. This was a show of power. "Get your goon off me."

Alexi waved him away.

"What do you want, Markov?"

He shrugged a shoulder. "I was just curious about Kat's special friend. She hasn't had one before that I know of. I care for her, you know. I just want to be sure she's safe and with the right guy. She can be impulsive, can't she?"

"What are you doing here? What do you want?"

"I'm confused. Now, I'm not a religious man myself, but a man such as yourself, a man of the cloth, is that how you say it? I thought you were celibate?"

My hands fisted.

"You're not breaking your vows, are you, Father?"

"What. Do. You. Want?"

"Well, I suppose that's your business." He reached into his pocket and withdrew an envelope. "I wanted to invite you to a party. But if you'd rather I leave…"

He stood, tucking the envelope back into his pocket.

"It's Kat's debut. I thought you'd want to be there. If it's allowed for a man of the cloth, I mean. But if you're allowed to fuck, then I guess a party would be all right."

He crossed the room, but when he was near enough, I put my hand on his shoulder to stop him. "What are you talking about?"

He looked down at my hand.

I didn't move it.

He looked back up at me. I had about four inches on him. "Tonight's party. Big show is a little after one in the morning. Trust me, you won't want to miss this." He took the envelope back out and tossed it onto the table, where I noticed a black box.

He walked on, and I looked down at the embossed, thick, silver envelope. I didn't even turn around to make sure they'd left. Instead, as soon as I heard the door shut, I reached down to pick it up and took the invitation out. Inside, the heavy, black card had a date, time, and place: tonight, very soon in fact.

I set the invitation down and opened the box to find a black mask with a long nose, like a plague doctor's mask of old days, but eerier. What the fuck?

Taking my phone out of my pocket, I dialed Lina's cell. I knew she wouldn't pick up. She probably couldn't. Alexi had her.

I picked up the box containing the mask and rushed down the stairs and out the door to hail a taxi. Giving him Club Carmen's address, I pulled my phone out and dialed Raphael. Lina had run out of time. I only hoped I wasn't already too late.

19

DAMON

The drive shouldn't have taken more than thirty minutes in heavy traffic, but tonight seemed to take longer than usual. We crawled along to the sound of horns honking and lights flashing in the distance up ahead.

"What's going on?" I asked the driver.

"Looks like an accident."

"Can't you take another route."

"How? Should I fly over the top of the rest of these assholes?"

"I don't have time for this."

"Newsflash buddy, none of us do."

"Fuck!" I threw some bills into the front seat and climbed out onto the street. Cars honked their horns, but they weren't going anywhere, so they could fuck off.

I wove through the lanes to the sidewalk and ran

as fast as I could toward the club. By the time I arrived, it was already midnight. The club itself was in full swing, but I saw the red carpet rolled out at the alley entrance with two men in black suits and white masks standing sentry.

Catching my breath, I dug my invitation out of my pocket and stalked toward them. One took the invite, looked it over, and handed it back. The other one opened the door. I stepped into a small room with black velvet draping every wall and even the ceiling. Tall cathedral candles dripped, and Gregorian chants whispered like warnings in the background. If dark and eerie was what Alexi was going for, he succeeded.

There were two other men inside, both donning long black capes and adjusting white masks over their faces. Two women wearing see-through silver dresses with every inch of visible skin painted silver stood to greet me at the door. They didn't speak, only took my invitation, looked it over, and led me to the coat check. I guessed this was where you got changed unless you were traipsing around Manhattan wearing a cape and a mask. Which, even here, would stand out.

I took off my coat and handed it to the girl. Silver flecks dropped as she moved, giving me a cunning smile and pushing what I assumed was a black cape along with the claim ticket for my coat across the counter. I tucked the ticket into my pocket.

The girl who'd walked me over gave me a similar smile and picked up the cloak. I guessed I was supposed to get into costume here. I slipped it over my shoulders, and the girl adjusted the clasp. I wondered if this was what Lina had done the night she'd come home painted gold. If she'd been half naked like this.

The girl took the box out of my hands, opened it, and held it out to me. I placed the mask over my face, and we walked toward the elevator. Two girls dressed like the one beside me exited the elevator, and my escort and I entered it. She pushed the button to the Penthouse, and we rode up in silence, each of us staring into our reflection on the mirrored doors. Her, beautiful, petite, delicate, me looking like the plague. Like the Black Death coming to claim its victims.

The doors opened to the same chanting as downstairs, only here, it seemed to be louder, more ominous. It wasn't a recording, which I'd assumed at first, but a group of men standing on a slight dais in a corner chanting.

Black draped the walls here too, but this room was larger, about as big as all of Club Carmen. Church candles dripped down long candelabras onto the black-and-white-veined marble floors. Every man here was dressed as I was, black capes and masks, some simple, some ornate. All terrifying.

There were women too. Their capes were a deep

purple, and they donned stiff, full-face masks. The ratio of men to women was about five to one, and there had to be well over a hundred people in the place.

The girl beside me gestured for me to step out. I did. She gave me that smile again, and when the elevator doors closed, she disappeared behind them.

If anyone turned at my entrance, I didn't notice it. They seemed to be absorbed in conversation, everyone with a flute of champagne in their hand. The servers were dressed in less than those who'd greeted me downstairs. They wore only high-heeled shoes, and silver chains hung from their hips and were clipped to rings on their nether lips. They flitted through the crowd with trays full of fresh glasses of champagne.

My hands fisted at the thought of Lina here among them, on display like this.

But I looked at each of the girls and didn't see her. I wasn't sure if I felt relief or more anxious. Alexi had said it was her debut. What in hell did that mean?

Taking a glass of champagne I had no intention of drinking, I began to weave my way through the crowd looking for her, knowing I wouldn't see her, not yet. Not until he wanted me to.

I checked for exits other than the elevator, but any doors were hidden behind the drapes. Alcoves led off the main room with sitting areas arranged, where small groups collected, laughing, talking. It was similar to the club below, but what was happening in those places was different. As time passed, the laughter grew louder, and it seemed guests broke into circles, some as small as three, others as large as ten. A throng collected around one particular recess, and when I went to it, I realized why. I don't know why it took me so long to see what tonight was. What it would become.

I turned my back to the moaning, groaning threesome and took a step toward where men in suits were setting up chairs across from a staging area where a platform had been erected.

I checked my watch. A little after one in the morning. I stood for a moment, noticing for the first time that although everyone wore a mask, many were similar but there wasn't a single one like mine in the room.

Of course. It made sense. Alexi would want me to be recognizable even with the mask hiding my face.

Casually, I turned back to where the lovemaking—no, it was fucking—was going strong. The woman was fully naked and on her hands and knees. She had one man in her mouth, the other behind her. The men, although still mostly dressed, had discarded their masks. They had carelessly tossed them aside. Moving quickly, I slipped mine off and replaced it with one of theirs, leaving mine it its place. It was a simple white face, nothing special about it. In fact, I now matched about half the men in the place.

A gong sounded, and heads turned. Mine too.

Chairs had been arranged. Two naked women knelt on either side of the gong, which stood on a wooden platform about two feet off the floor. A man wearing only some sort of loincloth and headdress stood before the women and sounded the gong again. People moved to take their places. I followed, choosing a seat along the aisle in the third to last row.

I had a feeling Lina was about to be debuted. But had she agreed to it or was Alexi forcing her? Was this what her plan was, and when Alexi learned about me, he wanted to make sure I witnessed her fall? Was it to disgrace her? Further humiliate her? Because she would be humiliated tonight, he would see to that. I had no doubt of Alexi's intentions.

Or was it to show her as some sort of whore to me? To force me out? No. It wouldn't be that. A man like Alexi Markov wouldn't waste his time on that sort of calculation. He was a thug. He'd use his fists. Or his goon's fists.

One more strike of the gong and the room fell into hushed silence. Darkness descended, any overhead illumination dimming so that only candlelight remained at the periphery of the crowd. A few moments later, a spotlight appeared on a door where a man entered dressed similarly to the guests, except he wore a bloodred cape. And his mask, which covered everything but his grinning lips, was the most elaborate of all. Alexi Markov. I'd know it from his walk, from the way he sauntered as if he were God.

Applause followed his entrance. Alexi gave a sort of bow and held up his hand for silence.

"Tonight, dear guests, is a special night indeed," he began.

I phased him out and peered into the darkness from where he'd come, but it was impossible to see. Refocusing on him, I waited as he continued to speak. I followed his gaze around the room, knowing he was searching for me. For the mask of the black death. We found it at the same time. The man wearing it sat two rows ahead of me.

After about five more minutes of Alexi spewing nonsense, a spotlight focused on the space just beyond the stage. Two masked men drew the black curtains apart and held them open. After a few moments, the first woman walked out.

My throat tightened to watch her and the dozen that followed her. All beautiful. All naked. All with iron bars on their shoulders, the weight of which made their backs bend. Their arms were spread wide and bound to the bars at the wrists. One by one, as they approached, I gazed at each of the woman, dreading the moment I'd see Lina. Wanting to get it over with. Wanting to know she was safe. Wondering how in hell I was going to get her out of here.

But she never came.

As each woman walked onto the stage, Alexi introduced them, turned them around, bent them over, then had them stand on a wooden block to begin the bidding. Although it made me sick, I knew these women were most likely hired for this purpose. Lina was not. And as the final bid was taken and the bidder disappeared behind a curtain where I imagined accounting took place, I grew more anxious, knowing Alexi was saving the best for last.

20

LINA

A Scold's Bridle caged my head.

But Alexi wasn't finished with me yet.

In fact, he'd only just begun.

I stood just on the other side of the curtains that shielded me from the room where I'd served Alexi's party not so long ago. I wore a long silvery-white evening gown that hung off my shoulders and draped low at the back. My arms were bound behind me with leather restraints at both elbows and wrists, forcing me to stand up straight, making my breasts jut out against the delicate silk, my nipples visible beneath it.

The shoes I wore were one size too small. I wondered if that was intentional. My skin still stung from the hot wax I'd endured to tear every hair—apart from that on my head—from my body.

But none of that mattered.

It all paled in anticipation of what was to come as the last of the women before me walked up onto the stage and was auctioned off.

Because I was next.

I wore the Scold's Bridle—a medieval device used to punish gossips, used to humiliate them. Heavy metal imprisoned my head, leaving my eyes to see, my nose to breathe. Inside my mouth, the bridle depressed my tongue, making it impossible to swallow, to speak. To scream. To beg for help from a gathering of people who would only revel at witnessing my shame.

"Walk." The man who stood guard commanded me. I startled and glanced up at him. He didn't meet my gaze, though. Instead, he kept his just beyond me, only nudging me forward when my legs wouldn't work.

The murmurs of anticipation ceased as I set one platform shoe into the spotlight, then the other. I stopped. My guard leaned down close.

"Walk."

When I met his gaze, they conveyed a silent warning. And so, I walked. Specks of silver dropped from my shoulders as I entered the room where Alexi waited for me at the center of the stage, where a sea of masked faces gave audible sounds of approval as I came fully into view.

My humiliation, it excited them.

"Ah...my pièce de résistance."

Every single person in the place brought their hands together in fervent applause, the sound deafening as it bounced off the marble floors. I looked at them, and terror gripped me at what I knew Alexi had in store. I would have screamed if I could. I would have run. But there was no way out, not for me, not this time. This time, I was finished. And all I could do was stand trembling and mute as I faced my fate.

I didn't hear what he said. I couldn't listen as bile rose up my throat and threatened to choke me.

Two women appeared out of nowhere and I felt the cool of metal against my shoulders. In an instant, they snipped the dress from me. Cool silk slipped down my body and pooled at my feet on the floor. I barely had a chance to look at it before I was turned in a circle. Displaced as Alexi spoke lewdly of my charms as I was bent double and I felt the arousal of the onlookers as if they were a collective, single body.

I tripped when I was hauled upright but somehow didn't fall. Alexi named an amount, and the first hand rose high, followed quickly by a second and a third and a fourth. It kept going, Alexi calling out numbers, bidders bidding. I struggled to wrap my brain around the fact that I would soon be raped.

The room began to spin, all the arms rising as each man or woman outbid the last blurring before my eyes, Alexi's voice lost amid the shouts from the guests. A final number was called out, and when it was, time seemed to stop. Everyone turned to the man standing. The one who'd just placed what I knew would be the final bid.

I glanced at Alexi, who studied the masked stranger, his expression one of pure hatred.

I didn't understand. Wasn't this what he wanted? Wasn't this how he wanted to punish me? Forcing this violence upon me?

"Sold."

I stumbled when he said the word, losing sight of the room as I almost passed out. Alexi caught me and the lights went down on the stage. He faced me, and once I was steady on my feet, he wrapped his hand around the back of the bridle to grip the lock and force my head backward.

The guests began to rise from their seats as the stage lights went down.

"I like you like this, Kat. Maybe I should have had you wear it when you played at the club."

I didn't miss that he spoke in the past tense.

When I made a sound and tried to break away, he tugged harder. It was a moment before he released me.

Two women reappeared to lead me away, a guard following close behind. Their hands were gentler than Alexi's as they walked me into a round room bare of furnishings, draped heavily with rich crimson curtains, large tiles covering the floor in a black-and-white pattern.

A man stood guard as a woman led me to the very center of the room, where they wrapped a leather cuff around one ankle and bound me to a ring in the floor. One of the women sprinkled a handful of rice at my feet. I found it strange, not comprehending at first.

"Kneel," she said.

Then I understood.

The women each held one of my arms to steady me as I knelt on the hard grains. They dug into my skin, and I knew they'd be agony soon.

I glanced over my shoulder at the guard who dismissed the women. He waited beside the door until, a moment later, it opened. Alexi entered, the grin on his face more terrifying than any mask he could have worn. He circled me once, stopping just in front of me, the bulge in his pants inches from my face.

"Good news. Your knight in shining armor has paid your debt. Or should I say priest in shining...cassock?"

I glared at him.

He laughed at his own idiotic joke and rubbed his length through his pants. Just as he reached for the zipper, the door opened and a masked man entered.

21

DAMON

Blood pumped so hard in my ears I couldn't hear myself think.

My fisted hands shook as I looked at her there, kneeling on the floor, arms bound at both elbows and wrists behind her, attached at her ankle to a ring on the floor, naked, the Scold's Bridle muting her.

She trembled as tears slid down her face, and I wondered how many of those others, how many of those fucking bastards who'd bid on her, would find her tears arousing. Find their pleasure in her pain.

"Ah," Alexi said, turning to me. "Here he is, our happy buyer."

I looked at Lina's terrified eyes, turned back to Alexi, and peeled the mask off my head. I could tell he wasn't surprised at seeing me.

"Bought and paid for," Alexi asked. "Just like the whore she is."

Lina shook her head wildly but I couldn't look at her. Not if I wanted to save her.

"Bought and paid for," I said through gritted teeth, barely recognizing my own voice.

Rage burned the blood coursing through my veins, and I knew if I didn't get us out of there fast, I'd kill him. I'd fucking kill him.

"Keys," I said, holding out my hand.

He reached into his pocket to retrieve a set. "Shall I take off the bridle? You'll want to use her mouth, I presume?"

"Bought and paid for, Alexi. She's mine. Give me the fucking keys and get the hell out."

"Touchy," Alexi said, feigning offense.

His eyes gleamed, though, and I knew he was enjoying this.

"I suppose for the amount she cost you can have the bridle. Maybe you'll want to keep her in it. Becoming, isn't it?" he asked, shifting his gaze to her.

I stepped to him before the guard could get near me, grabbed the collar of his shirt, and shoved him backward against the wall. Two hands landed on my shoulders, but I was in Alexi's face and I wasn't finished. Not nearly.

"Her debt is paid. She's finished with you and your father. Is that clear?"

I heard the door open and more soldiers come inside. Hands gripped my arms.

"Is that fucking clear?" I asked as they dragged me backward.

Alexi snorted and adjusted his collar. He approached, and when he was an inch from me, he drew his fist back and punched me hard in the gut.

"You don't give the orders here, *Father*."

He hit me again, but I didn't care, not as long as he wasn't touching Lina. But he returned his attention to her too soon, bending down so he was at eye level with her.

"I don't know if you heard, but there was a terrible accident at the prison," he said in a loud whisper, feigning upset.

Lina's puffy, reddened eyes widened as Alexi pulled her hair hard, tugging her face upward.

"A riot, they said. Luckily, only one prisoner was killed."

Lina tried to say something, but she couldn't form words.

I tried to break free, but Alexi stood and turned to me. "Work him over."

He gave me a wicked grin before tossing the keys onto the floor before Lina's knees. "While she watches. And when you're done with him, take what you want from the whore."

He walked to the door. Someone opened it for

him, but before he left, he turned back to face us one more time.

"Make sure he watches that part. They're free to go after that. If either of them can walk, that is."

Alexi walked out the door, leaving three guards behind. I looked at Lina's desperate face, watched her struggle helplessly with her restraints. I didn't think at that point. I didn't hear anything either, at least I didn't hear anything apart from rage.

It does have a sound, rage. It's like an all-consuming, wordless, formless sound, something like chaos. Like a fucking battlefield. I wonder if that's the sound of blood boiling.

Whatever it was, it filled my ears. The room around me receded, leaving only Lina there, Lina kneeling, chained, and at their mercy. Lina on her knees beneath their hands.

I let that thought fuel me, those images burn into my retinas, and somehow, some way, with a wild roar, I fisted my hands and heaved my arms forward, dragging the men who held me from behind me, gaining power as I listened to her cries, to their angry voices, and flung them into each other, skull crashing against skull, until they released me, dazed and confused. While they stumbled, the third man's fist collided with my jaw. Pain momentarily flashed like lightning before my eyes, but I didn't have time for pain. I didn't have time for anything. Because this was it. This was it for her.

I pounded my firsts into three of Alexi's men before me, one after another after another as they landed hit after hit on me, my face, my gut, my kidneys. I struck back every single time until finally, somehow, I gained the upper hand.

After the first one fell away, I loomed over the other two, backing them against the wall. I dragged down the drapes hanging there, tore the material to reveal the brick wall beyond. Taking them both by the hair, I smashed their faces against it, hearing bone break, feeling blood splatter onto my face, my clothes.

I don't know how many times I did it. I only know at some point, even after they went limp, I continued, unable to stop. Not until hands closed over my arms and dragged me backward, forcing me to release them. I kicked at one lifeless body before I stumbled back over another, slowly coming back to reality, someone shouting orders, the sounds of screams from beyond, the feel of cool metal circling my wrists.

I turned to Lina as men in black, FBI written boldly across their protective gear, stormed the room, disappearing behind a curtain where a door had been. One man bent over Lina, and again, I tried to tug myself free of those who held me now. They wouldn't hurt her. I wouldn't let them hurt her. I wouldn't let them fucking hurt her.

"Lina!"

The man straightened, pulling the Scold's Bridle from her, freeing her. I followed her gaze to his and redoubled my efforts to free myself, failing again as he stood at his full height.

"Maxx?" Lina managed.

It was Alexi's man, the one who'd been at my apartment.

"Get these things off me!" I ordered, twisting against the two who held me, handcuffed, dragging me farther and farther from her. "Lina!"

Maxx moved behind her, and I would have lost it then. Hell, I had already lost it, hadn't I? Didn't at least one man lie motionless on the floor just feet from me? He was dead. I knew dead, and he was it.

"Don't fucking touch her!"

But he didn't, not like that. He undid her bonds and helped her to stand. Granules of rice sprinkled onto the floor, but too many were still etched into the flesh of her knees. He then picked up the cape—mine, it must have fallen off during the fighting—wrapped it over her shoulders and let her come to me.

"Damon," she wept, burrowing herself into me, holding me tight, tighter than she'd ever held me before.

I couldn't move my own arms to wrap her in them, to drag her away from this bloody scene, from the screams coming from the outer room.

"Take them to the hospital," Maxx said. "Don't let her out of your sight." He gave the room one more glance, me one more look, and disappeared into the outer room.

22

LINA

I'm responsible.

I sat alone in an office much like those I'd seen on *Law and Order* and those sort of shows on TV, not sure how long I'd been here. I wore no watch, and there wasn't a clock in the room. They'd brought me here once I'd gotten the all clear at the hospital. I wasn't hurt. No one had laid a finger on me.

Damon, though? I couldn't get the image of him fighting out of my mind. I couldn't stop seeing fists pounding flesh, heads colliding with a brick wall. Blood splattering. Staining Damon. And the man on the floor. The one who would have beaten Damon. Who would have raped me. Who had lain, unmoving, on the floor of the penthouse.

No. More likely he now lay in a drawer in the morgue.

Shit.

I'd fallen asleep once. Or more times. I didn't know. I just knew that I'd startle awake, my head on the table, eyes feeling like they were plastered shut. There weren't even windows in the room, so I could see the sun. Or the night sky. Or anything.

Standing, I went to the door for the thousandth time, but for the thousandth time, it was locked. They hadn't let me in to see Damon at the hospital. When we'd arrived, they'd taken us to separate rooms, and we'd both had a police escort. Several.

They'd handcuffed Damon. Did that mean he was in trouble? He'd defended himself. He'd defended me. I could testify to that. But who would believe me after my visit to Sergei which I'm sure was logged somewhere.

I pulled at my hair, wearing another circle in the ragged wall-to-wall carpet, until, finally, a lock turned in the door and it opened. I stood and watched as Maxx and another man walked in holding a file that had to be at least two inches thick.

They closed the door behind them, and Maxx faced me, looked me over.

I was wearing a pair of gray sweatpants, a matching sweatshirt, and a pair of ancient sneakers, all of which were too big. I'd folded the pants up several times to keep them up, but it was either that or be naked, since I didn't have any clothes on when I'd arrived at the hospital.

"Ms. Guardia," he said, setting the file folder down and taking a seat.

He sounded so different, looked so different. He was still wearing black from the raid, his muscles bulging beneath his shirt. His eyebrows were furrowed, and his expression serious.

When I'd known him as Alexi's bodyguard, he was always distant, as if he didn't see or hear a thing. I'd always known the opposite was true, but this was…weird.

"It's Lina," I said, taking back my old name.

He sat back in his chair, surveying me, not betraying a single thought.

"I don't understand," I started. "You work for Alexi."

He shook his head. "I'm a federal agent. Maxx Carson. I work undercover, and in this case, I needed to get close to Alexi Markov." He cleared his throat. "I'm glad you're not hurt. Physically, I mean."

"But Damon's hurt. No one will tell me what's going on."

"Damon Amado will be fine. He had a couple of bruised ribs and a fractured wrist. Not surprising, and quite lucky, considering."

I exhaled, a huge weight lifted from my shoulders. But then I realized something.

"Am I in trouble?"

He studied me. Christ, it was unnerving.

"You know that Sergei Markov was injured in a riot at the prison yesterday?"

"Injured? Alexi said he'd died. Or he'd suggested it." Although he'd never named Sergei now that I think about it.

"He's recovering. His injuries are serious, but he'll pull through."

He watched me. Was it wrong that I felt relieved he hadn't died?

"Am I in trouble?" I asked again.

"We have questions. For now, that's all."

I nodded. Did they know about the journal I'd kept rather than turning it in? Was that what he had questions about?

"What was your relationship with Sergei Markov?" he asked.

"He was my employer at Club Carmen until he was arrested and Alexi took over."

Maxx raised an eyebrow. "That was all? He gave you an apartment to live in free of charge, bought you clothes—"

"How does this matter?" How does my stupidity matter?

He leaned back in his seat and folded his arms across his chest. "It matters. Especially given the fact you visited him a few days ago in prison. Especially given the fact that three of the people named in the file he gave you turned up dead in the last year, and another has gone missing."

"Dead?"

"Dead."

"You were in that file too."

He gave me a half grin. Before I could say more, I heard commotion outside, and the door opened.

"I'm sorry, Maxx," a woman said.

An older man in a three-piece suit walked inside and set his briefcase on the table between the agents and myself. He took out a card and handed it to Maxx, who took it. He then handed me one.

"Reginald T. Lewis. My client is no longer answering questions."

"Client?" I asked.

Mr. Lewis pulled a chair over and sat down beside me. "Your brother-in-law, Raphael Amado, arranged for representation."

"Raphael?" Shit. He knew? That had to mean Sofia knew too. I shook my head. "Representation? Am I under arrest?"

Maxx leaned forward to answer before Mr. Lewis could speak. "No. You're not. We're looking to answer some questions, Ms. Guardia. That's all. I've been involved in this investigation for longer than you've known Alexi Markov, and unless you're going to tell me something I don't already know, you have no reason to have an attorney present."

"I'll ask you not to intimidate my client," Mr. Lewis said.

Maxx gave him a look but sat back in his seat.

"I'm okay to answer questions," I said to all of them. "I want to." But first I had one for Mr. Lewis. "Raphael hired you?"

"Yes. A colleague is a mutual friend."

"Is he...coming here?"

"No. You sister is unable to travel, and he won't leave her at this stage of the pregnancy."

"She's okay, though?" How long had it been since I'd talked to Sofia?

"As far as I know, she's fine."

Maxx cleared his throat. We both returned our attention to him.

"You visited Sergei Markov in prison a few days ago."

"Yes. I went to him because I was afraid of what Alexi would do, how far he'd push me. He thought I owed him money. But you know that part. You were there." He'd stood by when Alexi had slapped me. He'd caught me and stood me back up to take more. "You let him hit me."

He had no reply, but the look in his eyes told me he hadn't forgotten.

"Sergei told me he'd help me. He said he'd wipe out my debt and get Alexi off my back if I told him if those people in that file were at Alexi's party. But they're dead or missing, so I don't understand."

"He was getting a message to Alexi. He knew Alexi would have you followed. I did the following.

That's why my photo wasn't in the folder when Alexi received it."

"He used me?"

Maxx looked at me like I was an idiot. And I guess to him, I was.

"He was sending his son a message. Having my photo among the informants they both knew to be informants would make Alexi suspicious."

"He wanted to help Alexi?"

"He wanted to protect his interests."

"But Alexi tried to have him killed?"

He didn't answer me. "Sergei Markov also gave you a healthy payout," he said instead.

"I told him I didn't want anything. He just included the money in the file. I never planned on keeping it."

"That so?" he asked sarcastically.

"It is. You don't have to believe me if you don't want to, but it's all still there. And it's the truth."

"The money doesn't matter, Lina," Mr. Lewis said. "You can't help it if someone gives you a gift, even if it is from someone like Sergei Markov."

"Where's Alexi?" I asked.

"Safe and sound in a prison cell, where he belongs."

"But why would he try to have his father killed? Especially after Sergei tried to help him."

He replied to my question with another one of his own. "Mr. Markov mentioned something during your visit to the prison." He paused, perhaps for effect. "He mentioned ties to your grandfather."

How did he know what we'd talked about? It must have been the prison guards. Sergei was cocky. Had he gotten sloppy?

I glanced to the attorney, who put a hand on mine and patted it.

"You don't have to answer any more questions." He turned to Maxx. "I believe Ms. Guardia has been more than generous sharing what she knows. I'm sure the night's events have taken their toll on her and she'd like to get home. Rest."

"Sergei and Alexi Markov are both trying to make a deal, Ms. Guardia. They'll tell whatever lies they need to tell to save their own necks. Father against son, son against father. And they might just get away with it, if they can cast enough doubt. These are two very bad men we're talking about." He began to take out photographs from inside the file. I only looked at one before having to turn away, my breath catching at the gruesome sight.

"Oh, come on. That's not necessary," Mr. Lewis said about the photos.

Maxx ignored him and spoke to me. "Your lawyer is right. You don't have to answer any questions. I can subpoena you to testify under oath. It would just be a hell of a lot easier to do this now." He leaned toward me. "You're not in trouble. We're interested in putting the criminals behind bars. Not you."

"Lina—" Mr. Lewis started.

"No," I said, meeting Maxx's gaze. I had to come clean with all of it. I had to finish this. I'd withheld evidence. Had any of the people in the photos he kept laying out before me died because of that? Because I'd been trying to protect my grandfather and inadvertently protected the Markov's? "My grandfather," I started. "He's an old man." Tears burned my eyes. "I don't want him to get into more trouble."

"Tell me what you have exactly, and I'll see what I can do."

"We'll make the deal before she shares any information. Immunity for my client, for her grandfather—"

"I have a journal. I kept it when I handed over the other two. The ones that showed where the money Grandfather stole had come from. Where it went."

Mr. Lewis muttered something under his breath.

"Go on," Maxx said.

"The name Markov is mentioned several times. Sergei, or maybe both of them, worked together with my grandfather."

"Where is it?"

"In Italy. At the house in Tuscany. I hid it in the chapel on the property."

Lewis threw his arms up at this, and Maxx sat back in his seat. "Make the calls."

Maxx's colleague had already stood.

"Thank you," Maxx said. "I need you to stick around in case I have more questions. Can I trust you'll do that?"

I nodded. "Can I see Damon?"

"I'll have someone drive you back to the hospital."

"Not necessary. I'll give my client a ride."

"My apartment. Sergei said it was bugged. Was it?"

"No. Not by us, at least."

So, he'd lied to me. He'd used me and lied to me. "Can I go back and get some clothes?"

"The apartment is off-limits for now. My men are going through it in case more evidence has been hidden there."

"And Damon, he's not in trouble, is he?"

"Self-defense is not a crime."

I exhaled an audible breath. "I'd like to go."

Maxx nodded. "That's fine." He reached into his pocket and withdrew a cell phone. "This is for me to be able to get a hold of you. It's either that or a holding cell, and I don't want to do that to you."

I took it, looked at it, and nodded.

We all stood.

"Ms. Guardia."

I had reached the door when Maxx spoke. I turned around.

"I didn't like that he raised a hand to you. If he'd done more, I wouldn't have allowed it."

I wasn't sure what he expected. If he thought I'd tell him it was okay. Because it wasn't. Instead of acknowledging his comment, I turned to leave with Mr. Lewis.

When we got outside, I could see it was morning from the position of the sun.

"How long have I been in there?"

"Thirty-six hours."

"That's more than a day."

He only raised his eyebrows and gave a knowing nod, then drove me to the hospital, catching on quickly that I didn't want any conversation when I sat silently in the passenger seat as he tried to make small talk. When we arrived at the hospital, I climbed out.

"Thank you, Mr. Lewis."

He reached out to hand me a card. I hadn't taken the one he'd given me at the FBI building.

"It's no trouble, but you'll want to be careful with the FBI. They suspect everyone is a criminal, no matter how open or flexible they may try to make themselves appear. Your brother-in-law is paying a hefty sum to retain me, so I'd like to be sure you'll contact me if they approach you directly."

"I don't have anything to hide, Mr. Lewis. I just laid out all my cards."

"It's how they'll play those cards that worries me."

I wanted to get inside. I didn't want to stand here having this conversation. "I'll call you," I promised, taking the card.

Once inside, I went up to the fifth floor and Damon's room. At least I thought it was his room, but when I pushed the door open, an old man slept in the bed Damon had been in. Panicked, I backed out and double-checked the room number before turning and looking both ways down the hall for the nurse's station. I practically ran to it.

"Excuse me. The man in room 523, Damon Amado, where is he?"

The nurse held up her finger to signal she'd be with me in a moment and finished her phone call, which sounded more like a private conversation than work.

"Excuse me!" I tried again.

Giving me an irritated look, she hung up the phone and cocked her head to the side, not bothering to smile. "How can I help you?"

"Damon Amado. He was in room 523 yesterday. Where is he?"

She clicked through several screens on her computer before answering. "He was discharged a few hours ago."

"Discharged?" Thank goodness. "Do you know where he went?"

She leaned back in her seat. "It may surprise you to learn this, but we're not babysitters here, Miss."

I ran back to the elevators, taking one down and heading out, realizing as I got to the street that I didn't have my purse or wallet, and no part of me wanted to call Mr. Lewis for a ride. It would be an hour's walk to the church. Wrapping my arms around myself, grateful it wasn't snowing or raining as this jogging outfit barely kept the cold out, I headed away from the hospital and toward the church.

23

DAMON

I sat in the front pew of the church, staring straight ahead at the crucified Christ. My vision blurred, and I wasn't sure anymore how long I'd been there. I needed food and sleep, but I couldn't move from this spot.

Lina had been taken to FBI headquarters for questioning. I'd tried to go to her this morning once I was discharged but hadn't been able to get past the reception desk. I'd left a handwritten message for her but didn't know if she'd get it. If they'd bother giving it to her.

Raphael had arranged for an attorney, so at least she wasn't alone. And I'd needed to come back here to the church, my mind awash with the events of the night before.

I'd saved Lina, but in the interim, I'd killed a man. I'd beaten him to death.

I slipped a rosary bead from one finger to the next but didn't say prayers. It wasn't quite conscious, that. The beads, they were habit. Years of training. I stared ahead at the altar, at Christ's dead body.

I had taken a life. This repeated in my head. But that wasn't the most upsetting, unsettling thing.

I wasn't sorry.

Not then. Not now.

All I could think of, in fact, was wrapping my hands around Alexi Markov's throat and squeezing the life out of him.

Was this bloodlust? Was this what happened once you killed? You grew a craving for more?

He'd put Lina on a fucking auction block, muted her with the bridle, bound her with leather and chains. He'd stripped her naked for all to see. He'd ordered her rape.

A sound came from deep inside my chest, a rumble, like that of an animal. Something feral. And I couldn't stop thinking about how very differently all of this could have gone. About what could have happened to her.

I had spoken with Father Leonard once I'd arrived at the church. It hadn't been a confession. Not at all. I'd just needed to come clean. To tell the fucking truth. Say it out loud.

I'd told him what had happened. How I felt about it. How I wanted to decimate Alexi Markov.

How I wasn't sorry for killing a man. How I would do it again to protect her. I told him that I'd fucked her.

I'd fucked her.

He was either incredibly well schooled at masking his emotions or he hadn't been surprised, at least not by the final piece. I guess that part *was* a sort of confession. But didn't you have to be sorry for it to count as confession? All these years at seminary, and I'd never once considered that.

I wasn't sorry.

Not even close.

I was angry. No. Not only that. I raged. That bloodlust still burned through my body.

The church doors opened, and I straightened, listening to the footsteps as they came toward the altar.

I knew it was her. I felt it.

She stopped, but I didn't look up. Instead of slipping into the pew, she knelt before me, turned her face up to mine for a moment, then lay her head down on my lap and wept silent, heavy tears.

I had stitches on my face, just beneath my eye and across one eyebrow. I wore a splint around one wrist, and my ribs were bandaged, but that she wouldn't have seen. My shirt hid that damage. Blood still stained my clothes, mine and theirs.

At least it wasn't hers.

Her matted, knotty hair needed to be washed, to

be brushed. Her body needed to be scrubbed. To take away the filth of that night. To banish any trace of it from her skin. From her mind.

She wore a horrible, oversize gray sweat suit and an ancient, filthy pair of sneakers too big for her feet. I reached to touch her head, stroking her hair. She turned her face up to mine, her eyes ringed with remnants of dark eye makeup. It made them look even more hollowed out. Her skin seemed to have lost the color she'd picked up in Florida. She looked pale and tired instead.

The image of her wearing that iron mask, the Scold's Bridle, flashed across my mind's eye, and it made me fist my hands.

"Damon." She must have felt the shift inside me.

I leaned down, took her face in both hands. It was cold but I didn't care about that. I raised her to stand as I stood.

"I'm so sorry," she said, again and again, over and over. "I'm so, so sorry."

"Lina," I started, my voice hoarse, dark, as if it weren't my voice, but someone else's. I walked her backward toward the altar. She tripped when the backs of her feet hit the first of three steps leading up. It didn't matter, though, not for what I needed to do. What I would do.

I couldn't stop looking at her. I couldn't stop thinking about what I'd almost lost.

My grip on her face hardened. It was like I needed to know she was real. Tangible. I kissed her. I'm not even sure what kind of kiss it was but a need built inside me separate of desire, of want or passion.

I shifted my gaze from her to the altar, to the crucified Christ above.

I'd thought I'd chosen. I'd thought I was doing the right thing. But everything blurred with her. All those lines I should never have crossed I now stood firmly on the other side of.

She yelped when I lifted her off her feet, ugly, oversized sneakers slipping off her when I hauled her over my shoulder and carried her out of the church. Away from here and up to my room.

I didn't speak. Neither did she. I set her down before my bed, gripped the waistband of the hideous pants and shoved them down over her thighs, off her legs. I pushed her to sit on the edge of the bed.

I felt crazed, enraged still, and yet, as I looked down at her startled face, her confused eyes, the slit of her naked sex, all I could think, all I could hear, all I could feel was the blood pumping into my cock, my erection thick and hard and needing to be inside her, to come inside her, here, like this.

I lay her back and undid my pants, shoving them and my briefs down only as far as I needed to grip my cock.

"What—"

"Quiet."

"Damon—"

When she tried to rise, I pressed a hand across her chest and slid inside her folds, tight, not yet ready for me. But I didn't care. I wanted to hurt her, just like before. Just like when I'd punished her. I wanted to fucking hurt her because I was so fucking angry.

She made a sound, but I lay my weight on top of her and covered her mouth with my hand.

"Take it. Take me."

I drew back and thrust in hard. Sweat broke out over her forehead. Her eyes closed, and she panted beneath my hand. I withdrew and did it again, harder, watching her as I took her, as I hurt her.

Her hands lifted to my shoulders, and I drew mine from her mouth, setting them on either side of her head. Her nails dug into my sore, bruised flesh as she began to moan, her passage slickening.

She cried out when I thrust again. I'd never fucked angry before, and it felt good. Good to own her like this. To know I hurt her. To know taking her like this, it made her mine. That she was fucking mine. That it took that night, that terrible night, for my eyes to finally open.

Lina's hand touched my face. Her touch was soft, gentle. Opposite what I was doing to her.

I returned my gaze to hers. I rose up a little, took

hold of her right knee, and pushed it back alongside her torso. I glanced down at her cunt, her little asshole, all of her exposed to me.

Like it should be.

Like it always should have been.

I slid out of her pussy, and for a moment, she looked confused. My cock was drenched in her juices and I gripped it, guiding it to her tight hole and pressing there, rubbing against her until she opened and took the head of my cock.

I met her eyes again. They'd gone a little wide, and I liked it. Liked her panic. Liked her giving this to me despite that panic.

"I don't care if you come," I said, pressing deeper into her, the passage so tight and so fucking warm.

Her nails broke the skin of my shoulders, her eyes closed, her teeth caught her lip as I claimed more of her, finding my rhythm, taking her ass inch by inch until I was seated to the hilt.

I stilled there, savoring her heat, the knowledge I was inside her here, so fucking deep inside her.

She made a sound, and I looked at her. She moved, rubbing her clit against me, and as I watched, she moaned as she came—fuck, it took her moments to come.

Her cunt leaked, wet my belly and thighs, the walls of her ass pulsed around me while I watched her, watched her in ecstasy, memorized her face in this perfect moment, that millisecond before I thrust, fucking her ass, hearing her cries as I took my anger out on her, all while watching her come again and again before, finally, I reached my peak and stilled, throbbing, releasing, emptying inside her ass, filling her with my seed, filling her with me.

24

LINA

I lay limp in Damon's arms. I still felt him inside me, his cock inside my most secret place, his cum there, still. I wanted to keep it forever, a piece of him, forever, inside me.

Damon seemed different. If I expected him to be sorry or to feel guilty over what had just happened, well, I knew he wasn't. In fact, he seemed determined, sure of himself. Not at all confused.

"Damon?"

He turned to me, looking me over from head to toe. He hadn't picked up the shoes they'd given me. They were still lying on the floor of the church.

As if he hadn't heard me at all, he stripped me fully naked. It wasn't erotic or harsh or gentle. It was mechanical.

"Lie down on your belly."

Even with his come still inside me, my clit swelled at the order. I swallowed.

Damon walked toward the bathroom but turned to me at the door when I hadn't moved from the spot.

"Do as you're told, Lina. I know that's not your strong suit, but that's changing. Now. Lie down on the bed on your belly. I need to clean you."

"I can clean myself," I said, understanding what he meant to do, my words quiet as heat flushed my skin.

"Hmm." He turned his back. "Lie down," he said, ignoring me altogether.

He disappeared into the bathroom. I heard water running. I slowly moved to the edge of the bed, lying down as he'd said. He soon followed and took a pillow from the bed.

"Lift your hips."

I looked at the wall opposite to where he sat and did as he said. He slid the pillow beneath my hips, elevating them.

"Is this necessary?" I asked.

"Yes." He settled on the bed. "Spread your legs."

I did, feeling aroused again even as I tried hard not to let his stuff leak out of me, knowing I'd die of humiliation if that happened.

"Good girl. Reach back and spread your cheeks."

"Damon—"

"Do it."

I reached slowly back to do as he said. I spread myself open for him and stared straight ahead, mortified.

"Now look at me."

I shook my head. I didn't want to see him, didn't want him to see me. Not like this.

"I said look at me."

Reluctantly I turned my head, so that I lay facing him. He met my gaze then purposefully shifted his to my ass.

"Things could have gone so very differently."

He rubbed the warm, soapy cloth over that most private place he'd just used.

"It didn't have to come to what it came to. I'm so grateful that you're safe, that you're not hurt, and at the same time, I am so fucking angry with you."

"I didn't have a choice, Damon. Alexi forced me—"

"I gave you a choice! *I was your choice.*"

"You left!"

"I told you I'd help you. I'd get you out of this mess."

I lowered my lashes. He was right. He had.

I heard him take a deep breath. Maybe he was counting to ten.

He rubbed the washcloth over me. I groaned, twisting away, but he gripped my hip, stopping me.

"No. Keep your eyes on me."

When I didn't move, he slapped my ass. I

jumped, more startled than hurt, and lay my other cheek on the bed so I could look at him. He still wore the blood-splattered shirt, and the stitches on his face looked painful.

"I want you to understand something," he started, taking his time with his words. "What happened to you last night—I can't think of it without feeling sick. The thought of you up there, unable to speak, bound, naked in front of those…"

His lip twisted in revulsion

"In front of those monsters." He slammed his fist against the headboard, leaving a dent in the ornate wood.

"If you'd been hurt—"

"I wasn't. You saved me." A tear slid from my eye, down over my nose, and onto the bed. I knew how close we'd come to him not having saved me. I knew what would have happened then. To him. To me.

"You answer to me from now on, do you understand?"

I nodded.

"You will stay here with me, and I will decide what happens going forward with the investigation, with everything. Including a call to your sister explaining everything."

"Damon, I can't do—"

"Including a call to your sister, explaining every single fucking thing."

I nodded, unable to hold his gaze.

"But first." He returned his attention to my ass. "Spread your cheeks." I had dropped my hands but now spread them again for him.

He rubbed the cloth over it before setting it down between my spread legs and removing the pillow from beneath me.

"Pull your knees up to your chest."

"Damon, please."

He petted my head, then took a fistful of hair and twisted it back. Gentle and…not. It was him. All of it was him.

"Is my come still inside you, Lina?"

I swallowed hard. He knew it was, he just wanted me to say it.

"Answer my question."

"Yes."

"I will know every part of you. Even this. I'm going to watch it slide out. Now draw your knees up and keep your eyes on me the whole time. There are more embarrassing ways to do this if you'd prefer."

"Please, Damon—"

"Relax your muscles."

Slowly, I did as he said, feeling equal parts ashamed and aroused, knowing this was an act of submission to him, to what he wanted, knowing this little humiliation, it was as much for me as for him. This was his power over me. It was my yielding it to him.

And so I did. I kept my eyes on his as I relaxed

my muscles and watched his face as his seed dripped out of me, sliding warm over me as it fell onto the washcloth. I saw his cock tent against his pants as he watched. And when he met my eyes and I held his gaze in this, my punishment, something changed between us.

The shift was small, but important. Something weighty. We belonged to each other in a way we hadn't before. It was whole and complete and final.

"I love you," I whispered.

He smiled.

When it was over, he rolled me onto my back and put his hand on my sex. Eyes locked on mine, he rubbed my wet pussy, my clit and kissed me.

It was tender, gentle. It was love making. And I gave myself to him as I came again, tongue on tongue, never not touching.

We went into the bathroom after that where Damon stripped off his clothes. That was when I saw the bandages around his middle. He ran water in the tub, checking the temperature before plugging it.

"The water's hot. Too hot. But I need you clean. I need to scrub off yesterday's filth."

He climbed into the tub. He let me look at him, at his damaged body, before stretching his arm out to me, palm up.

I realized what was different then. Up until this point, he'd always put my needs first, he thought of me first. He was doing that now too, but differently. On his terms.

"Come here, Lina."

Snapping out of it, I placed my hand in his and stepped into the tub. The water scalded. It *was* too hot, but I'd adjust, get used to it. I lowered myself down slowly. He slipped in behind me, cradling me between his knees.

"How did you get here?" he asked.

"I walked."

"Walked? From the FBI office? Without a coat?"

"No. From the hospital. The lawyer Raphael arranged drove me to see you when they let me go, but you'd already been discharged." I paused, and my eyes filled up at the returning memories. "You're hurt because of me."

"I'm fine. It's nothing."

"Your bandages—"

"Can be replaced."

He picked up a loofah and began to scrub my back. It felt good, at first, but it got rougher and rougher. I sat through it, though. I didn't move. Instead, I watched his face in the reflection of the mirror on the opposite wall.

"Sergei isn't dead," I said, unsure if I should bring it up.

"That's too bad. Turn around."

I shifted so I faced him, splashing some of the water out of the tub as I did.

"Damon, are you okay?" Was he in shock? After the killing? I wanted to ask, to talk about it, but knew I needed to leave that to him.

He stopped and looked at me. "I'm not sorry."

"What?"

"I'm not sorry for having killed a man. For injuring the others. In fact, all I can think about is wrapping my hands around Alexi's throat and choking the fucking life out of him too."

"Damon—"

He began to scrub me again, his gaze far-off. I let him.

We didn't speak until he'd finished. He let the water out of the tub and climbed out, grabbed a towel, and wrapped me in it, drying me before getting one for himself. He dried himself off then dropped it so he stood naked.

"Let's sleep," he said. "I think we both need to sleep."

He drew the curtains closed and led me to the bed, where he lay me down before climbing in beside me and wrapping a big, heavy arm over me. His breathing leveled out almost immediately. I lay there for a moment, in the safety of his arms. In the warmth there. In the feeling of home.

"Thank you," I said. "Thank you for coming for me."

He tugged me closer. "Sleep, Lina."

25

DAMON

Early the following morning, I went to a shop nearby to pick up basics for Lina to wear until the feds let her back into the apartment to get her things. I now sat across the table from her while she and I listened to the phone ring at Sofia and Raphael's house.

Raphael hadn't told Sofia anything. That was apparent from the way she answered the phone, from the small talk she exchanged with Lina. From her surprise at hearing me with her.

"I'm confused, I thought you were in New York City, Damon? Is it my pregnancy brain that's got this wrong?" Sofia asked.

"I am in New York City. There's nothing wrong with your brain. But I've kept something from you that I shouldn't have," I said.

"It's not his fault," Lina chimed in.

"What's going on?" Sofia asked. I heard Raphael in the background, and we listened quietly, not quite hearing the whole conversation but parts of it, especially the part when she asked him how long he'd known and why he hadn't told her.

"It's not Raphael's fault either, Sofia. It's mine. I swore Damon to secrecy. Blackmailed him, really, into keeping my secret."

"Are you okay, Lina?" Sofia asked, concerned.

Tears welled in Lina's eyes, and the tip of her nose reddened like it always did when she was about to cry. But she drew in a deep breath and sat up straighter.

"I am now. Raphael, can you hear me too?"

"Yes," my brother answered.

"I'm sorry I made you lie to Sofia."

"You didn't make me do anything I didn't choose to do, Lina. I don't like it, but it was for the best. I'm glad you're coming clean now," Raphael replied.

"Have the police been out there yet?"

"Police?" Sofia asked.

"Yes," Raphael answered. "They found the journal and took it. I'd guess it's either in the FBI's hands or close to it by now."

"What journal?"

Lina explained to Sofia how she'd kept one piece of evidence that was too damning to their grandfather. Sofia listened in silence.

"That's one of the reasons I came to New York City. It was all I could think about, that journal, what it said inside. The name Grandfather mentioned: Markov. So, I found him. I needed to see him for myself. Make some sense of things."

Lina told her the whole long, sordid story, and Sofia listened in silence.

"What's going to happen now?" Sofia asked, her voice tight.

"I've hired Lewis to defend her, if it comes to that. He'll be present as she's questioned," Raphael answered.

"They can't arrest you. You were sixteen," Sofia said to Lina.

"I don't think that's what they want," Lina said. "I just want to be sure Grandfather isn't in more trouble."

"He made that trouble. That trouble had nothing to do with you!" Sofia snapped. "You made it yours."

"He's our grandfather," Lina said softly.

"And look what he's done. Destroying our legacy wasn't enough. He nearly got you—" she broke off.

Lina wiped her eyes as Raphael came on the line.

"When are you bringing her back home, Brother?"

I looked at Lina. "That's up to her, once she gets the all clear from the FBI." I wouldn't drag her anywhere, wouldn't force it. That was how she'd gotten into this mess. It was one of the first things she'd said to me. Everyone did everything for her own good. Me too. "I'll be here with her, though. She won't leave my sight until this is resolved."

"I'm not allowed to fly," Sofia said quietly, sniffling. "I wish I could be there with you, Lina."

"You belong there, Sofia," Lina said. "You have to think about the babies. You're still not finding out if they're boys or girls?"

"The way they kick, I'm sure at least one will be a soccer player," Sofia said.

Lina smiled, her first authentic smile in a long time. "I can't wait to meet them," she said.

"Me either," Sofia replied.

The cell phone Maxx had given Lina rang. She looked at it, then at me.

"We have to go," I said. "We'll call again later."

"Damon?" Raphael said.

I picked up the phone, disabling the Speaker option. "Yes?"

"You and I need to talk."

I'd told him about the dead man.

"Let me take care of Lina first."

"All right. If you need anything else—"

"I won't hesitate."

We hung up. I turned to Lina, who nodded her head and told the person on the other line she'd see them in an hour. She then hung up.

"It's Maxx. I can get into the apartment to pick up my things."

Her relief showed on her face.

"I appreciate the clothes you bought me, but honestly, you dress me like a nun."

I smiled. "I'm not used to buying women's clothing." I'd picked up a knee-length skirt and an oversize sweater. What I'd paid attention to were the undergarments: a lacy pair of deep red panties and matching bra.

"And they have the journal. They're running some tests on it now, I guess, comparing it to the evidence they already had. Maxx will be here in forty-five minutes. He'll take me to the apartment, then to their offices for more questions. I should probably call Mr. Lewis."

"I think that's a good idea."

"I don't have anything to hide, Damon."

"I know that, but he knows the law. It can only help you to have him there. And I'll be there too."

"I don't know that they'll allow that."

"I don't care." I checked my watch. "I need to head downstairs to talk to Father Leonard."

Father Leonard stood sweeping the church floor when I walked in. I had a feeling he'd been waiting for me.

"Damon," he said, setting the broom aside and walking toward me.

"Father." From when I'd first met Father Leonard, he wasn't what I'd expected. I had a feeling, though, that Gavin had put great thought into sending me here to him rather than anywhere else.

"I was just finishing up," he said. "Thought I'd get a cup of coffee. Would you care to join me?"

"I'd like that."

We walked out of the church and to the coffee shop down the street. We ordered our usual drinks and took a table at the back. Father Leonard studied me.

"How is the girl?" he asked. He had to know Lina was with me.

"Better."

"I'm glad. And, how are you?"

"Better too."

When I stopped at that, he sipped his coffee then started again. "Gavin is a clever old man, you know. He has a keen eye. Did with me too. He made sure I understood there was no sin in sowing my wild oats before I decided to take the final step. At least, for me, it was that. I have a feeling it's different for you."

I held his gaze and I knew. In fact, I had no doubt. "I love her."

He nodded, smiled. "When will you let Gavin know you're leaving seminary?"

I ACCOMPANIED Lina to her apartment. The FBI had been thorough in their search, even floorboards and cupboards had been torn up. What they hoped to find I wasn't sure.

Lina didn't say what she felt at seeing this, but I had a feeling she'd never been at home here. Not with Sergei, not with Alexi.

She packed up her personal things, stuffed three duffel bags full, while Maxx looked on, arms folded across his chest. We then drove to his office, where she'd be questioned again. Mr. Lewis met us there, and when I entered the interrogation room, Maxx opened his mouth, saw my expression and closed it again.

"The journal is authentic," Maxx said. "And it proves the Markov's connection to your grandfather."

"What will happen to him? My grandfather, I mean?"

"He's cooperating with us," Maxx said, seemingly annoyed about it. "He'll cut a deal to turn over Sergei."

"Only Sergei? What will happen to Alexi?"

"We'll use this to make sure Sergei turns over evidence on his son."

"Will he do that?" Lina asked.

Maxx sat back and looked at us in turn. "Both men are guilty of many things. If I can put them both away for thirty years, I'll take it over putting one away for fifty and letting the other go free."

"Is Lina safe?" I asked.

"That's one thing I need to talk to you about. We'd like you to testify against Alexi Markov. Tell the jury you were essentially held against your will, put up for auction. Give them an idea of how that evening went. Sergei and Alexi aren't the only two we're prosecuting. We picked up several others during the raid. Several others who were willing to buy the use of your body without your consent."

Lina's face paled.

"No," I said.

"It would—"

"I said no."

"Those people...they're horrible. The things I saw them do..." she shook her head, then faced Maxx again. "But that night, they wore masks. I won't be able to identify who bid on me."

"That won't matter as much as you telling us and the jury your experience, painting the picture. Both that night and the other night when you served drinks."

"And what about her safety?" I asked. "Wouldn't this be putting a target on her back?"

"She'll be under our protection."

"Under your protection? You stood by while she was essentially kidnapped by Alexi Markov. Hell, you helped him."

"The operation—"

"Fuck your operation," I said and stood. "Lina."

Lina slowly rose to her feet. Lewis stood too and began to pack his briefcase.

"I wouldn't want to subpoena you if I didn't have to," Maxx called out when we got to the door. "You have means to get out of the country, a home to go to. I'd prefer a cooperative and willing witness rather than a flight risk."

"Are you threatening my client?" Lewis asked.

"What if...can I go back to Italy? I'd like to see my sister," Lina asked. "If I agree, I mean."

"Lina, you're not testifying," I said.

Maxx ignored me and focused on Lina. "You're not under arrest. And if you're a cooperating witness, I don't see why not, although protection there is out of my control."

"She doesn't need your protection," I rebuked.

"With all due respect, one man may not be enough for the Markov army," Maxx said.

That night flashed before my eyes. "With all due respect, where the fuck were you and your men when Markov ordered her gang raped?"

The attorney cleared his throat as Maxx and I stared each other down.

"I'm sure you both mean well," Lewis said.

Maxx took in a deep breath and leaned back in his seat, blinking.

"My brother and I have resources. I'll keep her safe."

"Ms. Guardia, think it over. Decide for yourself.

You can put these people away or let them free to hurt others."

"Isn't that your job?" I asked him. I opened the door. "Let's go."

26

LINA

"Maxx was just doing his job," I said later that night as we walked back to Damon's place after dinner.

"He knew all along what Alexi planned to do with you, and he went along with it. He was willing to have you become collateral damage."

"I don't know his intentions or what he thought, and honestly, I don't care. We're safe. Alexi's behind bars."

"And now the FBI wants you to testify against him and a slew of Russian mobsters."

"Maybe I should. I can't be afraid of them, and if I can help put them away, shouldn't I do it?" I paused, glancing away, remembering. "You weren't there for the other party, Damon. You didn't see what they did."

"I don't care about them. I care about you."

I pulled my hand out of his and drew back. "Why do you care? You're leaving anyway."

"What?"

"You're leaving in six months. The church will expect you back."

"I'm not going back. I told Father Leonard this morning."

"I don't understand. You'd decided."

"I'd decided wrong."

"What?" Had I heard right?

"I'm yours, Lina. If you'll have me."

"What?"

"I'm leaving seminary."

It took me a long minute to find my voice. "You mean it?"

He smiled. It wasn't an easy smile and I knew what this decision cost him but for a moment, for one single moment, I didn't let myself think about that part. I leaped into his arms, my chest swelling with happiness.

He was choosing me.

Damon caught me in his arms, laughing. And for a brief space in time, I thought this was it. This was our happy ending. Didn't we deserve it after everything? Had we paid our dues? Was it enough?

But before he'd even set me back on my feet, the phone Maxx had given me rang.

Damon registered it first, but my smile vanished soon after his. When I didn't move, Damon did, taking the phone out of my pocket and swiping to answer.

"Yes."

"Mr. Amado, this is Maxx Carson."

Although he didn't have the phone on speaker, I could hear Maxx clearly.

"I have some information I thought Ms. Guardia would like to have."

"What information?"

"Is she there?"

"What information?"

"Her grandfather is being moved."

I stared at Damon who remained silent.

"Don't worry, nothing's happened. He's healthy as a horse." Maxx cleared his throat. "For now, at least."

"What the hell does that mean?"

"He'll be transferred to the prison where Sergei and Alexi Markov are being held."

"What?"

"The decision isn't mine unfortunately."

"Is this because she won't testify against Alexi?"

"The two are unrelated."

"Right."

It was quiet for a long moment and I had the feeling he'd planned this.

"I may not be in a position to stop the transfer, but I can provide security for your grandfather."

"Let me guess. You'll want Lina's cooperation in exchange for that security."

"Cooperation is always appreciated, Mr. Amado."

"Fuck you, Maxx. Fuck you."

I grabbed the phone out of Damon's hands and walked away.

"I'll do it. I'll testify. But you need to swear he'll be protected. If he's hurt—"

"Lina," Damon said.

"You can't let them hurt him." I couldn't be responsible for hurting my grandfather again.

"I'm glad to hear it. Why don't you come into the office tomorrow morning, and we can talk through the details. Leave your boyfriend at home."

"This isn't right. He's an old man."

"It may not be right, but this is life. And your grandfather is no innocent bystander. There's a reason he's in prison. I'll see you tomorrow morning, Ms. Guardia." He hung up.

"I'll call Lewis. See if there's anything we can do," Damon said.

"I'm tired, Damon."

"Let's go upstairs. You can lie down for a bit—"

"Not that kind of tired. I'm tired of this. Of life being like this over and over and over. Am I being punished? Is that what this is? Is it because of what I did to my grandfather? Or is it because of us? Because I stole you?"

"You did the right thing. Your grandfather is a criminal, Lina."

"He's still my grandfather."

Damon sighed. "And you didn't steal me. I chose you."

"Your God is vengeful."

"No, he's not."

"How can you say that after everything that's happened to you? To your family?"

"Because the alternative is too terrible."

27

LINA

Damon, Mr. Lewis, and I met with Maxx the following morning to go over my testimony. The trial, which I'd thought would be a long time coming, had been scheduled for four weeks from now. I wasn't sure if I was glad, relieved to have it sooner rather than later, or nervous. At least it meant I could go back to Italy, see my sister, sooner than I had planned. I could truly close this chapter and start over.

But there was one thing that I needed to do before I could do that. As much as I dreaded it, the time had come.

Maxx arranged for me to visit my grandfather later that week. Damon offered to accompany me, but I needed to do this by myself. I sat alone in the back of the car Maxx had sent, feeling anxious, my stomach in knots. I remembered the last time I'd been on this road with Stanley on my way to visit Sergei, who was still in the infirmary, although apparently no longer in critical condition.

Once inside, the procedure to see Grandfather was similar to the last time I'd been here. The agent who'd driven me presented some paperwork, then led me to the same room in which I'd met with Sergei. Only difference this time was, where Stanley had waited in the other room, the agent remained inside the room with me, standing at the door as I settled into the chair I'd sat in the last time and waited for Grandfather.

Damon had told me I didn't need to do this, that I owed him nothing. Sitting here now, I questioned my decision to come. This was the last place I wanted to be. He was the last person I wanted to see. But Damon was wrong. I did owe my grandfather something. I owed him the right to see me. To tell me to go to hell, if that's what he wanted.

The door I'd been staring at opened, and a guard walked in. Behind him, a man I almost didn't recognize followed.

My mouth went dry, and my heart raced even faster as our eyes met. My grandfather, Marcus Guardia, a figure I'd always remember as looming, ever present, all-powerful, now stood before me... looking different.

But not in the way I expected.

He seemed harder.

Meaner.

"Well, well."

He gave me a cruel grin.

"Katalina."

A guard placed his hand on Grandfather's shoulder, and my grandfather sat.

If I'd thought prison would have softened him, would have made him repentant or remotely sorry, I was wrong. I knew it from the look on his face, the tone of his voice. From the energy rolling off him, threatening to make me vomit.

"Cat got your tongue?" he asked.

I swallowed, and my hands shook. "No." I stared at his eyes, darker now.

"That's all you have to say after four years of silence? Not a single visit. No letter. Not even a postcard to an old man?"

"I'm sorry."

"For what, exactly?"

His question confused me, caught me off guard. "I'm sorry I didn't come to visit."

"No, you didn't. Neither did your sister. What ungrateful girls I raised."

"We're not ungrateful."

"No?"

I felt suddenly protective, defensive of my sister. I didn't care what he said about me, but Sofia wasn't here to stand up for herself. "What you did to Sofia was unforgiveable. I know what it cost her to attend your trial, to arrange everything for us when the bank seized the house, when the feds seized all our assets. You have no right to call her ungrateful. I'm just glad at how things turned out for her. That's a miracle."

He scowled. "A miracle, indeed. You bed the devil you'll raise his spawn."

"How can you say that? She's your granddaughter. They'll be your great-grandkids."

"Why did you come?" He made no attempt to hide his contempt for me. What had I hoped for? Expected? Whatever it was, it hadn't been this. "To get one final look before your friends put an end to me?" he continued.

"My friends?"

"Don't play the innocent. You never were. You're your mother's daughters, both of you." He leaned in close. "Tell me something. Did you bed the father first, then the son?"

My mouth fell open. "I bedded neither. And you'll be safe here. I agreed to testify against Alexi in exchange for your safety."

At that he laughed outright. "Who fed you that piece of bullshit?"

I almost answered, then stopped myself. All my life, I'd given him power over me. I'd been afraid as a child, cowered as a teenager, tiptoed around my whole life. That was finished. I was taking back my power. Now. "Are you remotely sorry for what you did? Do you take any responsibility for any of it?"

He snorted but had no response. He studied me, an accusation in his eyes. *Traitor*. I read it as clearly as if he'd said the word aloud.

"That's a no, I'm guessing," I said. "For four years, I've held onto that other notebook feeling guilty, feeling like I betrayed you for turning over evidence at all, wanting to spare you, wanting to not believe what was in that last one. Hoping it wasn't possible you knew of those things that happened. Thinking you couldn't have known. I thought coming here, I'd see you as a different man, one who was sorry for some of it at least. But you're not. Not even a little." I took a deep breath.

"You grew up with a silver spoon in your greedy little mouth. You're the reason it's all gone, and I'm in here."

"I'm not the greedy one, and you're wrong. I'm not the reason you're in here. *You* are."

He had no reply, and I continued, asking something I wasn't sure I wanted the answer to.

"Did you ever love us?"

That seemed to take him by surprise. It took him a few moments to answer. "We're family, Katalina."

Why did his answer wound me still?

I stood. "I'm glad I agreed to testify. I'm glad you'll be safe."

He chuckled at that.

"I'm glad I'll help put Alexi Markov away for a very long time."

"Just be careful. He may be behind bars, but he's in no way less dangerous. If he's anything like his father, and I have a feeling he is, he won't be one to overlook a betrayal."

I ignored his warning. "I'm glad I came, but I won't be back." At that, his expression changed, eyes softening a little, but perhaps it was the desperation I glimpsed in them that made me think that. "For what it's worth, I don't wish you harm. I never did. And I did love you," I said. Tears filled my eyes, and I turned my back. "I still do." I walked quickly to the door.

"Lina," he called out when the agent who'd escorted me reached to open it.

I turned to find him on his feet, prison guards flanking him. He looked a little less tall, his shoulders not quite as wide, his countenance not as foreboding.

"I wish things had turned out differently," he said.

I had no reply. He could have meant a hundred different things. This was, after all, the very worst way for things to have turned out. He could have been talking about getting caught. He could have been talking about Sofia and the deal he made with Raphael. He could have been talking about anything at all. All I could do was believe what he meant was that this, us, our family, that he perhaps wished that had turned out differently. Better. I didn't know.

Without a response, I walked out, the agent at my heels.

28

LINA

The next two days passed without a call from Maxx and tonight, we were going to see Jana and the band. Damon had run out to pick up a few things at the grocery store, but just as I stepped out of the shower, he approached, his expression serious.

"What is it?"

He held an envelope out to me. "Not sure. Someone slipped it beneath the door downstairs."

I took it and read my full first name, *Katalina*, typed neatly across the front.

We didn't exchange words as I opened it. The note was a printout, not handwritten.

You wanted to keep me safe. Now I'm keeping you safe.

That's all it said.

I read it twice, three times. My brain made sense

of what it said, I understood, but I didn't want to. I handed it to Damon but didn't wait for him to read it. I walked away to get dressed. A moment later, I heard the tearing of paper. I looked up to watch as he ripped both the envelope and the note apart, walked into the bathroom, dropped the pieces into the toilet, and flushed them away.

Our eyes met. It was a moment before I spoke. "I want to book our tickets to go home."

He didn't miss a beat. "I'll call Lewis in the morning."

Neither of us mentioned what had just happened.

"Why Lewis?" I asked.

"See if he can put some pressure on Maxx to hurry this along. Alexi's dead. No reason for you to testify now."

We stood like that for a moment, studying each other. We had a secret now. One neither of us would mention ever again.

I turned to get dressed.

After slipping on a tight-fitting black dress and a pair of high-heeled black pumps, I faced him again. He hadn't moved.

"Ready?"

Damon's gaze burned as it raked over me. It made me think of the last time we'd gone to the club.

He nodded once, his expression never relaxing.

We went down the stairs and out the door, hailing a taxi about half a block away. Always the gentleman, Damon opened the door for me, let me in before climbing in himself and giving the driver the address.

The band was already playing when we arrived. It was close to midnight. The club was packed, the scent of beer and sweat and just too many people assaulted all my senses upon entering.

"We don't have to stay long. I just want to see Jana. Tell her I'm leaving soon."

"That's fine. Want a soda?"

Shawn the bartender walked over toward us.

"Please."

He ordered, and Shawn gave me a wink, then got our drinks. Damon turned his back to the bar and sipped his beer.

"Do you remember the last time we were here?" he asked.

"Yes." I also remembered how the night had ended.

He slid his gaze over me. "You danced with those men to get my attention."

I cocked my head to the side. "The way you responded, I already had your attention."

"I asked you if you liked it. Liked men looking at you. Wanting you. You never answered."

"I thought you were flirting."

"Do you?"

He didn't miss a beat, his expression unchanging. Hard.

That was the first time he'd acted more like a possessive boyfriend than a brother-in-law or a man soon to be a priest. He didn't like men looking at me. I didn't want to tell him I did like it. I especially liked watching him when they did. It was the look he got in his eyes. The knowledge that he wanted me. That he couldn't stand even another man's eyes on me.

I shrugged a shoulder, stuck the straw in my mouth, and watched people dance.

He took my drink and set it down next to his. With one arm wrapped around my waist, he led me to the dance floor, then through it, past the bathrooms, toward an isolated alcove.

"This would once have been a confessional."

He pushed me into the tiny space and drew the dark red curtain closed.

"Now it's a make-out room."

He shoved me against the wall and smashed his mouth against mine, his fingers at the hem of my short dress.

"Is that why you brought me in here?" I asked when he leaned away.

He grinned, hiking my dress to my waist and drawing the crotch of my panties aside to drag his fingers through my folds.

"No."

He pinched my clit between thumb and forefinger, making me bite my lip as I raised one leg up and wrapped it around his hip.

"Then why?" I asked.

Damon unzipped his jeans and shoved them and his briefs down far enough to free his ready cock. He hoisted me up so that I straddled him. I wrapped my legs around him and, keeping his gaze on mine, he slid me onto himself.

"I brought you in here to fuck you."

He thrust as I clung to him.

"Damon—"

"That's not all."

He kissed me feverishly, gripped the hair on the back of my head, and forced my face up.

"I want every man in here to know you're mine. I want my scent on you. My cum inside you."

I let out a moan as he pulled harder, hurting me a little, and, at the same time, making me feel so good.

"I'm just not sure if I should come in your cunt and let it drip down your thighs as you dance, or make you kneel here and fuck your face. Come down your throat."

I dripped around him, more turned on by his words than I wanted to admit.

"Or maybe I should turn you around," he said, pulling out of me and spinning me so I faced away from him. "Bend you over, and fuck your tight little ass." He pushed the crotch of my panties over and put a finger over my asshole. "Make you keep my cum inside you all night."

I let out a small moan, curling my fingers in his hair, but then he stilled inside me, watching me closely.

"I like this tight little hole, Lina," he said, placing my hands on the low bench. I arched my back as he crouched down behind me holding my panties aside to lick me from hole to hole, before circling my ass with his tongue.

He straightened, pushed his thumb into me.

I moaned as I looked back at him.

"This hole it is," he said, one corner of his mouth rising. He slid into my pussy with a deep sigh and I felt my muscles hug him tight.

He thrust once, twice, growing thicker, making me worry I wouldn't be able to take him in my tight hole, but when he drew out and brought the head of his cock to my ass, I wanted it. I wanted him inside me there. The thought of him coming inside me there turned me on like nothing else.

"Push against me," he said when my body resisted and when he wrapped one hand around to rub my clit, I closed my eyes and did as he said, knowing someone could walk in on us at any time, hearing the sounds of the club, of so many people so close and us here, us in this private place. Damon fucking me here, like this.

"That feels...so good." There was a little pop and

my muscles relaxed, letting in the thickest part of his cock.

Damon moaned, leaning over me to kiss my neck.

"I love your ass, sweetheart. I love how it looks when it stretches to take me."

I looked back at him wishing I could see, too. I arched my back for more. I wanted it hard.

"Fuck my ass hard, Damon. I want to feel you come inside me."

He muttered a low *fuuuuck* under his breath before he gripped both hips and did what I wanted. What we both wanted.

29

DAMON

Lina was dead on her feet by the time we got back to my apartment.

"I'm exhausted," she said as we climbed the stairs.

I paused.

Something felt off.

"Stay," I told Lina, leaving her half way down the stairs.

"What is it?" she asked, suddenly alert.

I put a finger to my lips and slid the key into the door. I unlocked it, and saw the shadow as soon as I opened the door.

Lina had followed me up and gasped when she saw the figure.

I stood studying the man's back as he blew cigarette smoke out before flicking the butt out onto the alley below. He dropped the curtain closed and turned to face us.

"Zach?"

I flipped on the lights. My younger brother stood beside the window. He slid the hood of his sweatshirt off and shifted his glance from me to Lina, who slipped her hand into mine, her eyes wide on him.

The last time I'd seen Zach had been when he'd had a three-week leave two years ago. Those three weeks had been cut short. I still remembered that. He looked different now. Older than his twenty-four years. His dark hair wasn't cut quite as short as was required by the military anymore. He wore black from head to toe, and I could see the ink of a bright new tattoo creeping up one side of his neck. From the scruff on his face, he hadn't shaved in more than a week. His eyes had lines around them that hadn't been there two years ago, and a scar split his right eyebrow in two.

I waited until Zach turned his attention to me and felt a sense of relief when a cocky grin softened his features.

"Well, well, Brother. You got good taste. But I'll be honest, you bringing home a girl is about the last thing I expected to see."

"Who is this?" Lina asked.

Her worried eyes fell on me.

"This is my kid brother, Zach." I closed the door and took a step toward Zach, looked him over. He was built big, like Raphael and I, but he seemed to have gotten bigger, his eyes harder. "They teach you how to break into people's houses in the military?" I asked, giving him a grin, trying to hide my worry as I drew him in for a hug.

"Among other things," he said, hugging me back tightly, then releasing me. He cleared his throat and looked beyond me to Lina.

"This is Lina Guardia." He was clearly waiting for more. Lina stepped forward and extended her hand, which he took.

"Nice to meet you, but you gave me a hell of a scare," Lina said.

I moved to the kitchen to take two beers out of the fridge. "Lina, why don't you go have a shower."

"Oh, I can do that later—"

"Now's good," I said to her.

I handed Zach a beer and set mine down on the counter. She opened her mouth to protest, but I raised my eyebrows, very aware of Zach's eyes following us.

She glanced from me to Zach.

"Fine," she said, then turned to walk into the bathroom.

Once the door closed and the shower ran, I picked up my beer and took a seat on the couch.

"First Lina now you."

"What?"

"What kind of trouble are you in, little brother?"

He was. He had to be. No word in months, then he turns up in my apartment, standing in the dark like some criminal, looking like he hasn't showered in too many days.

"Nothing I can't handle." He gestured to the bathroom. "Church allow girlfriends now?"

"I'm leaving the church. No. I left. We're only here until a few things get straightened out. Then I'll take her home. She's Sofia's sister."

"Ah. That's why she looked familiar."

Zach had met Sofia on that trip home two years ago.

"The Lord works in mysterious ways," he added. The sarcasm in his tone grated. Neither of my brothers had cared much for my choice to join the seminary.

"What's going on, Zach?"

He drew his hoodie over his head and tossed it aside, then sat down and set his empty bottle on the coffee table. I saw that the tattoo I'd glimpsed on the side of his neck wrapped around his arm. It was a two-headed snake, mouths open, fangs bared. But more disturbing was the skin of his other arm. Bumpy and scarred. As if it had been burnt.

"How do I say this?" he started, asking himself the question. "You might get a letter in the coming weeks telling you I'm MIA or died in action or some bullshit. Well," he faced me. "It's just that: bullshit. I got fucked, Brother."

"MIA or dead?"

"Mission went wrong. Most of my men died. Thirteen of them, to be exact." He shook his head. "I should've died."

"How? When?"

"About three months after I saw you. A mission the American public will never hear about."

"Where have you been for the last nearly two years then?"

"Like I said, I should've died. The less you know the better."

"Are you in hiding?"

He thought about that for a few moments before answering, then shook his head. "No, not hiding. Just got into the country a few days ago. I'm here for answers."

"Zach—"

"Tell me about the girl."

He clearly didn't want to talk about whatever was going on with him. It seemed everyone around me had secrets. "I ran into Lina by accident. She was supposed to be in Chicago. Turned out she'd moved to New York City and had managed to get herself a job with a Russian mobster."

Zach whistled. "You know how to find them. Mind if I grab another one?" he asked, motioning to his beer.

"Help yourself."

He got a beer out of the fridge and returned. "So, a Russian mobster?"

"And his son. That's almost taken care of now, but she's got Feds tailing her. Security, they say. They need her testimony. And since I'm getting the feeling you don't want to be found—"

"That's who the two buffoons across the street are. They're doing a bang-up job protecting her."

He touched his bottle to mine in a mock toast.

"You left the church for her?"

"I wasn't yet ordained." Why did I always feel defensive about it, like I needed to explain this piece? Why did it matter?

He studied me. "You love her." It wasn't a question.

The shower switched off, and we both turned to the bathroom door. Zach swallowed half his beer.

"I need to get out of here." He reached into his pocket. "I just need you to do one thing for me."

"Anything."

He handed me a sheet of paper with a name and a long series of numbers written on it.

"I need money wired into this account. My share of the family business."

"That's a lot of money."

"And you can't transfer it out of my account in Italy. They'll track that. I need it done differently. I'll pay it back."

"I don't care about you paying it back. Who's they?"

"Less you know, the better, brother."

"I want to help you, Zach."

"This'll help me. Can you do that?"

"Yeah," I said reluctantly, wanting more. Wanting to do more. "I'll figure out a way."

He nodded. "Thanks." He looked around. "I need to get out of here."

"It's the middle of the night."

"Best time for disappearing."

"Zach—"

He looked at me. "I just need to shower. Shave my face. I must look a sight." He ran a hand through the scruff of his jaw.

I didn't deny it.

"Can I borrow some clothes? A cassock, maybe?"

I studied him, knowing his mind was full, already on what he felt he had to do. "Anything you need."

"Thanks." The bathroom door opened, and Lina stepped out wrapped in a towel, a cloud of steam behind her.

"I'm pruny," she said. "Do you need me to go back in?" She made a face.

Zach smiled, but I was too worried to. "No," I said as Zach and I stood. "That's fine." I turned to my brother. "Go ahead in. Take whatever you need. I'll get some things together for you."

He nodded and patted my arm before making his way to the bathroom. He paused when he neared Lina, admiring the ink on her arm, shoulder, and back.

"Nice."

"Thanks. Yours too."

The bathroom door closed, and the shower switched on. Lina came to me. "What's going on?"

"I'm not sure exactly. I need to pack some things for him, in fact. Can you maybe get some food together for him?"

"Sure. I'll make a couple of sandwiches."

"Thanks." I took my wallet out of my pocket as I headed to my closet, glad I had a few hundred dollars in cash to give Zach until I got that money transferred for him. Lina helped me pack for him and, not half an hour later, my brother said good-bye and slipped out the door looking like a different man —clean-shaven, the clothes he'd had on in the trash can, wearing one of my suits, a long dark coat, and carrying a duffel bag of my things, including a cassock, and the food Lina packed.

I watched him disappear into the night and wondered where he was going. Because I knew what he was doing.

Trouble wouldn't have any trouble finding him. Zach was going out looking for it.

30

LINA

Seeing Zach standing in the dark in Damon's borrowed apartment had scared me more than I'd admitted. I'd thought that was it. That Sergei had sent someone for me. It would be the safest thing for him to do, and it would be my punishment for having turned in the journal. For having lied to him about its existence at all. I guess it made me realize how vulnerable I was, because my grandfather had been right when he'd warned me about Alexi. Just because someone was behind bars didn't mean they couldn't get to you if they really wanted to.

Knowing this made me think.

Mr. Lewis called two days later to tell me Maxx had set up a time for my testimony to be recorded. Now that Alexi was dead, their case against the others had weakened. He couldn't make me stay indefinitely, given there wasn't a case to be prosecuted yet. Sergei was still recovering, but they'd had to move his trial date out by a few months and were still investigating Alexi's murder.

Damon booked us two one-way tickets to Florence for the end of the week, and I now stood by the window waiting for Mr. Lewis to arrive to take me to Maxx's office. Damon wasn't allowed to attend this one, but that was fine. He didn't need to hear all the details.

The first interview took three hours before we broke for lunch then reconvened an hour later for the rest of the afternoon. We had four days exactly like this, and I felt exhausted every night when Mr. Lewis dropped me back off at Damon's apartment

I answered Maxx's questions, reliving every humiliating moment on camera, even though he already knew much of it.

It wasn't until the final day that Maxx asked me the question I'd been waiting for. The one where I could, hopefully and without perjuring myself, let Sergei know I meant him no harm.

"So Sergei Markov hired you, coincidentally, because of your piano-playing skills?" he asked.

"He knew who I was when I got to Club Carmen. I was naive to think he wouldn't. We never discussed the details. I imagine he hired me because he wanted to keep an eye on me. I mean, I sought him out. And he knew I'd turned over evidence on my own grandfather. But he was never unkind to me, and I never saw evidence of wrongdoing on his part. In fact, I only realized he'd known who I was all along when I went to visit him at the prison in order to ask for his help with Alexi. And even then, knowing my financial dependence on his son, knowing I specifically told him I did not want his help in that area, he gave me money to get out of town and away from Alexi."

"After you did one favor for him. So, he gave you a job, truly, considering he paid you."

"No, his payment would have been to free me of Alexi. That's all. The money he sent, I didn't expect to keep it. And I know now he used me to send a message to his son about traitors and about you in particular. But as far as I was concerned, Sergei Markov only ever helped me, from the very beginning."

"Do you think he would want to "help" you enough to kill his own son?"

I leaned back in my seat, and although my heart raced, I crossed my arms over my chest and tried to appear relaxed. "You'd have to ask him that."

Maxx took in a deep breath and ended the recording. Now that Alexi was dead, Maxx was disheartened by the fact that much of Sergei's crimes would be hung on Alexi's corpse. Father and son were so entrenched, their business dealings so close, it was hard to say who'd done what. Even my grandfather's notebook named Markov. Never Sergei or Alexi. And, after Alexi's death, my grandfather stated that the majority of his dealings had been with Alexi, not Sergei. Maxx's attempt to blackmail me into testifying against Alexi had backfired on him.

The more I thought about it, the more I knew my grandfather had done what he'd done to reaffirm his loyalty to Sergei. He was saving his life while protecting mine. And after all was said and done, I guess Sergei would come out smelling like a rose while his son rotted in the ground.

"What's going to happen to Sergei?" I asked when only Maxx, Mr. Lewis, and I were left, and we were getting our coats on to go home.

"He'll be out of the infirmary this week and will be relocated to his cell. We have evidence against him, but not as much as I like." He seemed frustrated.

"What about my grandfather? Since he's cooperating."

He gave me a calculated look "No comment on his *cooperation*."

Maxx knew Grandfather was involved in Alexi's murder. He had to. But he couldn't prove it, I knew that much.

"How many years will Sergei get?"

"Hard to say."

Mr. Lewis snapped his briefcase closed before coming to stand beside me.

"Well, Agent Carson, I believe we're finished here."

Maxx looked at me.

"Yes. We are. Thank you, Ms. Guardia."

"Thank you," I said, shaking his outstretched hand.

"If I need anything else, I'll reach out to Mr. Lewis."

I nodded, anxious to leave, to walk out of this office, this building, close this door, and go home.

Home.

I was going home.

Damon and I were going home.

31

LINA

Early in the morning of the day of our flight, Damon's cell phone rang, waking us both. He answered as soon as he saw it was Raphael and spoke for a few moments, sitting up, switching on the light. His face grew serious.

"When?" he asked.

"What's going on?" My heart sank at his question. I knew what it was. What it had to be.

Damon held up a finger and listened to whatever Raphael was saying.

"What?" I asked again.

"Two girls, huh?" He smiled.

Relief flooded me. He hung up the phone and turned to me.

"Tell me!" I yelled in my excitement.

"You're an aunt. And your sister was wrong. No soccer players."

"That's sexist. Girls can play soccer."

"You know what, you're right."

"They're okay?"

"Everyone's fine. Raphael wanted us to come right to the hospital."

I was anxious for the whole flight. Didn't sleep a wink. The sun was just breaking the clouds in the horizon, but I didn't stop to take it in. After clearing customs and immigration, we quickly found a taxi and headed to Careggi Hospital in Florence.

Damon took over, speaking fluent Italian—something I'd forgotten he knew, since he'd grown up here.

"She says we can leave our bags here," he told me.

We had four between us. As he'd only gone to New York City temporarily, Damon only had one large suitcase of clothes and personal items. Looking at him take my things, though—two years' worth—that barely filled three cases, it felt strange. Like for the past two years, I hadn't been really *living*.

"Ready?" he asked.

I snapped out of it, suddenly anxious about seeing my sister. "How do I look?" I asked, pulling my sleeve down to cover as much of my tattoo as possible, wanting to show Sofia after I'd told her first.

Damon took my hand and drew me close. He

touched my neck, and I realized they'd see part of it there.

"You have nothing to hide, and you look beautiful. Happy, actually. It's good to see you happy."

I took a deep breath, nervous, and clung tighter to his hand, noticing how he didn't pull away. We weren't hiding. He'd said that. I guess he meant it.

We rode the elevator up to the third floor and headed to Sofia's room. Before we reached it, though, Raphael turned the corner holding what I guessed was a cup of coffee. He wore jeans and a T-shirt, just like he used to. His hair was ruffled, and it looked like he hadn't shaved in about three days.

He stopped short, and it took him a moment, as if he were surprised to see us. But then a smile spread across his face, and we crossed the distance, meeting in the middle. Raphael glanced briefly to where Damon held my hand but quickly returned his gaze to his brother's.

"So, you'll have a house full of girls," Damon said.

I watched as they hugged. It was a good hug. A real one. I took the coffee cup out of Raphael's hand when it splashed as Damon patted his back. Raphael turned to me, looked me over from head to toe, his eyes narrowing a little as they found the uppermost part of the tattoo, but then softening again as he hugged me. It was strange being hugged by him,

Damon's identical twin. That it could feel so different to being hugged by Damon.

"It's good to see you, Lina."

He held me at arm's length.

"It's good to see you, Raphael."

"Sofia's been trying to stay awake for you."

"I can't wait another minute. Where is she? And the babies?"

"This way." He led the way down the hall and pushed her door open.

Sunshine filled the bright, white room and spilled onto Sofia in the hospital bed. It took her a moment to register that it was us, just like it had Raphael, but in the next instant, she held her arms out to me. A huge smile spread across her face.

"Lina!"

I began to cry right away, leaning down to hug my sister, to hold her tight, so tight I realized just how much I'd been missing her. "I'm so sorry I've been so distant," I said, our tears blending on our cheeks as she pushed me back to look at me before wiping her thumbs across my face and drawing me back in.

"I'm so, so glad you're here and you're safe, Lina. I missed you so much. So freaking much."

"Sofia," Raphael said, coming around to the other side of the bed. "The stitches."

Sofia groaned, and I pulled back. She looked at Damon and beckoned to him to come. He hugged her, although more gently than I had, and I heard her whisper to him.

"Thank you for bringing her home."

"I know she's glad to be here. Only sorry we couldn't get here sooner," he said.

Once Damon stepped aside, she retuned her gaze to me and looked me over from head to toe.

"Don't they feed you in New York?" she asked.

I'd put on a few pounds but was still thinner than I'd been when I'd left two years ago. I hadn't realized how much weight I'd lost under the stress of having Alexi in my life.

"I was saving myself for Maria's cooking."

"She stuffed me for the last eight months, so it'll be nice to have her focus on someone else," Sofia teased.

"You're okay?" I asked, pulling up a chair, although I was anxious to see my nieces.

She nodded. "Yeah. The girls are early but healthy. You want to keep them inside you and growing and safe as long as possible," she said, her eyes reddening again. "You should meet your nieces."

She began to sit up, and Raphael instantly had his arms around her, helping her. He gestured to the wheelchair that Damon pushed over, and in a few moments, he'd settled Sofia in it.

"You know I'm not an invalid, right?" she said as he wheeled her out.

"I can't take care of my wife?"

She glanced up at him, and he leaned down to kiss her mouth. I was so happy to see them together, to see them still so in love. I squeezed Damon's hand as we followed them down the hall and into the unit where my nieces were along with so many others. The room was set up with cozy rocking chairs and pretty pastel pink-and-blue walls, ducks, bears, and balloons stenciled along every surface.

"It'll be at least three to four weeks before we can take them home," Sofia said as Raphael settled her around two tiny little things sharing an incubator, both with tubes in their noses, both wearing the tiniest diapers, their skinny little limbs pink, heads covered with tiny caps striped pink-and-blue. On their wrists they wore bracelets with their names and their parents' names on them. I noticed Raphael and Sofia had matching ones.

Sofia slipped a hand inside to touch one. "This is Elena, she came first."

I leaned over to look at her, and Elena squirmed, blinking twice although never quite opening her eyes.

"And this is Siena. She followed a few minutes later."

Siena turned her face toward the sound of Sofia's voice, but her eyes remained closed.

"They're beautiful," I said. "Perfect."

Sofia looked up at me. "They are."

"The tubes?" Damon asked.

Raphael looked at Elena. "To feed them."

We all stood around admiring these two tiny little miracles for a while, until Sofia yawned.

"You need to sleep," I said.

"I have been—off and on."

"When can you go home?" I asked.

"A couple of days. But we'll be back to see the girls every day."

"I'll come with you," I said. "I'll drive." I gave her a wink. My driving skills were horrendous.

"I'll drive," Raphael said firmly, turning Sofia's wheelchair around and leading us back to her room. Once there, he helped her back into bed and she asked me to stay a few minutes. Raphael and Damon left us alone.

I pulled up a chair, and Sofia studied me, her face more serious than I'd ever seen it.

"I was really worried about you."

"I know. I'm sorry."

"You should have told me about school. Told me about that other notebook. What did you think I'd do?"

I looked at the floor, ashamed of myself, angry with myself for having hurt her. But what happened, it needed to happen. "I needed to make my own peace with this. I never meant to hurt you. It's just that I got deeper and deeper into it before I knew it, and I couldn't involve you after that. You or the babies or Raphael."

"He can more than take care of us."

"I know that. He's like Damon."

"You saw Grandfather?"

"I did. And I think I've made that peace. He is who he is. And I do believe that, in his own way, he is remorseful." I didn't say more. Maybe I would one day, but not now.

Sofia nodded, took my hand, and pushed my sleeve up to take in the tattoo that enveloped my arm. "Wow, Lina. This is beautiful."

I felt my face redden, embarrassed at her praise. "I designed it myself. Wait until you see the rest of it."

She kept hold of my hand but returned her attention to my face. "And Damon?"

"He's leaving seminary. He won't ever be ordained."

She gave me a bright smile that turned into a yawn. "I need to hear this story from beginning to end."

"But you need to get some sleep first."

"Yeah." She yawned again, and her eyes fluttered closed. "I'm so happy now, Lina. I have my husband, my children, you, and Damon back home. I have everything."

Damon and Raphael walked in just as she

drifted off to sleep. I pulled the blankets up to her neck and stood.

"Should we go outside, so we don't wake her?" I asked.

Raphael gave me a smirk. "A marching band won't wake that one once she's fallen asleep."

I laughed. That was true. Sofia slept like the dead.

"Why don't you two go home, get some rest. Come back tonight. And bring some food," Raphael made a face. "It's terrible here." He reached into his pocket. "Take my car. It's easier."

Damon grabbed the keys. "Thanks. Need anything else?"

"A change of clothes would be nice. We'd only packed for Sofia, which was kind of dumb," Raphael said.

"Where are you sleeping?" I asked.

"They'll roll a cot in here."

We said good-bye, and I kissed Sofia's forehead before leaving. Damon and I gathered our things at the nurse's station. We headed to the garage, where Raphael's car was parked, and drove to the house. We didn't talk much along the way, both of us tired, relieved, taking in the surroundings. All the change. But he held his hand over mine, which rested on my leg, between shifting gears, and the closer we got to the house, the more right this felt, the more at home I felt. And just as he brought the car to a stop at the house, I turned to him and touched his face, pushing hair out of his eyes.

"Thank you so much for all you did for me. I honestly wasn't sure I'd ever be back here again before you found me. You risked your life, Damon." As I said it, the full weight of it, of that night at Alexi's penthouse, of Damon being held by Alexi's men, Alexi ordering his beating, my rape…it all hit me like a ton of bricks, and all of a sudden, uncontrollable tears began to fall from my eyes. I knew it was a much-needed release, a necessary thing, I just didn't expect it to happen like this, not after all this time, all that had happened since.

Damon wrapped me in his arms, pulling me in tight.

"You never have to face anything alone again, Lina. I'm here. And I'm not walking away ever again."

EPILOGUE 1
DAMON

Autumn

Zach had been in touch with Raphael via a brief letter posted without a return address, telling him only that he was alive and that he would be in contact as soon as possible. He'd been right about a visit from the United States Military. It hadn't been to me, but to Raphael. Since the apartment at the church wasn't registered in my name, officially, I didn't live there.

During their visit, they'd told Raphael that Zach's final mission had failed, and that they believed him to be either a prisoner of a terrorist group or, if he were lucky, that he'd already been killed. I'd previously talked to Raphael about Zach's visit, so he'd been prepared for the news.

We'd transferred funds to the account Zach had created under the alias Michael Beckham. It was more than he'd requested, as much as Raphael and I could give him. We both wished he'd let us help him, but after seeing him that day in New York City, I knew it was something he had to do himself. I just hoped he'd be safe doing it.

Over the last two years, as the vineyard slowly grew, the ash that blackened it was replaced by vibrant vines with leaves that sprouted as green as Lina's eyes. Fat, juicy grapes ready to be picked now weighed down each branch. Since Sofia and Raphael's second wedding ceremony, Raphael and I had also started working on the house—at least until I'd been sent to New York City. Lina and I moved into a separate part of the house.

Elena and Siena came home four weeks after they were born. To look at them now, no one would have ever guessed how small they were at birth.

"It's almost creepy how much like you and Raphael they look," Lina said one morning as she tucked a blanket over them. Sofia and Raphael had gone out for the day, their first time since Sofia had been put on bedrest months ago.

"What do you mean 'creepy?' They're gorgeous," I said with a wink.

She gave me a huge smile. "Well, they are that. I

just hope they don't get that Amado scruff on their jaws." Lina rubbed the two-days of growth on my face. We stepped out into the hallway.

I pulled her in and rubbed my cheek across hers. "You love my scruff, admit it."

"It's so scratchy."

I bit her earlobe softly, dragging it out. "I never hear you complain when I bury my face between your legs," I teased as we walked out into the hallway. The sound of too many people in the house drifted upstairs.

"I can't believe you were going to be a priest the way you talk," she said, heading to the stairs.

I laughed at that and we headed downstairs to join the workers as everyone prepared for the harvest, while Lina stayed inside with the babies. Having her for an aunt meant they were going to be very spoiled.

It was only after everyone had gone home after dinner and we'd put them to bed after one more feeding that we headed to the living room.

"I haven't heard you play in a while," I said, opening the fall of the piano and sitting down.

She slid naturally onto the bench beside me. "We won't wake the babies?"

I shook my head and kissed her as she set her fingers on the keys, already playing a quiet piece.

"This is what you were playing the night I first walked into Club Carmen."

She nodded, soft music filling the space.

"I knew it was you the moment I heard it," I said, my tone quiet, my gaze moving from where her fingers danced over the keys, to her face, so concentrated, almost lost in it.

"How?"

She didn't look at me.

"I heard it. And all I could think was that the music sounded like a heartbreak."

At that she shifted her gaze to me.

"You heard that?"

"Yes."

"I haven't played this one in a long time." She returned her attention to the piano.

"Did you compose it?"

She nodded.

"It's beautiful."

She played, and memory took me back to that night.

"Damon... Do you ever worry?"

"Worry?"

"About things. Your brother, for example. Zach, I mean."

"Of course, but I've also learned to be aware of what's in my control and what's outside of it."

"And he's outside of it."

"Yes."

She nodded, but I knew that wasn't all there was to her question. "What's going on, Lina?"

She gave a quick, sideways glance but concentrated on the keys. It took her a long time to speak.

"I don't want to mess this up."

"You won't." I studied her face in profile, saw how her eyes had misted over. "Lina, you won't." When she didn't stop playing, I twined my fingers with hers to make her stop and waited until she faced me. Silence descended around us, the only sound the night insects coming from the open window.

"There are only two things that would make me happier than I am right now," I said. She waited for me to continue. "One is having Zach here with us. Having him safe and at home." She nodded with a sad smile and almost pulled her hand out of mine. "And the second," I said, stopping her. I slipped my hand into my pocket to retrieve the small box inside. Turning it to her, I opened the lid.

Lina's eyes widened even more, and she blinked hard, as if unsure what she was seeing was real.

"What…"

"The second thing is this. You. Will you marry me, Lina?"

EPILOGUE 2

LINA

Christmas

"You look beautiful."

Sofia tucked one more pin into my hair as I took one last look at myself. "Ready?"

"I'm nervous," I said, feeling chilled and sweaty at once.

"I think that's normal. It'd be weird if you weren't. Oh!" Sofia rushed over to where she'd set a small box on the nightstand. "I almost forgot." She handed it to me.

"What is it?" Sofia looked beautiful standing there in the tight-fitting emerald-green gown she wore. She'd lost all the weight from pregnancy, and breastfeeding seemed to make her glow.

"Open it. Something old and new at once."

I took it from her and saw how her eyes had already reddened.

"You're not going to make me cry already, are you?" I felt the moisture of tears in my eyes.

"Don't worry, all your makeup is waterproof."

I took the lid off the small white box and pushed the soft tissue paper back to find inside the locket I'd given her the day Raphael had come to take her away years ago.

"Shit, you are going to make me cry." I dabbed at my eyes with a tissue.

"Open it. I took it to a jeweler to make a change to it."

With trembling fingers, I drew the locket out of the box and opened it. Inside, rather than the space for only two photos, were two more places. The locket was now like a tiny book with the addition. Inside was a photo of mom and dad, a family photo of Raphael, Sofia, Elena, and Siena, one of Damon, and a final one—which made me giggle—of Charlie as a puppy. "Charlie's a good addition."

"What? He's family too."

"He is." I touched the one of our parents before closing the locket and looking up at her. "Help me put it on?"

She took it and walked around behind me, fastening it at the back of my neck.

"Now you'll know mom and dad are watching too."

"Shit." I grabbed another tissue out of the box in front of me and handed her one.

A knock came at the door, and Raphael opened it. He looked amazing, as usual, and the thought that Damon would be waiting for me at the end of the aisle looking just like that made my belly flutter.

"You both look beautiful," he said. "Ready?"

"Ready."

I stood and faced Sofia, who drew the veil down over my face.

Raphael drove us to the chapel over the snow-covered fields. We'd had five inches last night. Although I wore a faux-fur white cloak, I shivered when we pulled up to the chapel on the property. It had been fully renovated and, I was glad to report, had a working heating system.

Since the chapel was small, the ceremony would be a family affair with those closest to us standing witness. I didn't mind it, and the only pang of sadness I felt was that my grandfather couldn't be here. I had come to terms with the fact that I'd never be able to turn my back on him, no matter what, and we'd begun to write letters. I'd even sent him an invitation, and he'd sent his congratulations.

Raphael walked Sofia and me to the church and signaled for the music. Once it began, he pushed the door open. Everyone stood, and I got my first look at Damon, my soon-to-be husband.

I was wrong. He wasn't as beautiful as Raphael.

He was more beautiful.

And as he stood waiting, Sofia took her place at the front of the church and everyone turned to me. Raphael tucked my arm into his and smiled down at me.

"I'm glad he chose you," he said.

"Me too."

I didn't stop crying from the moment Damon took my hands, and all through the ceremony, from the lifting of my veil, to the exchanging of the rings, to the saying of our vows, until the priest pronounced us husband and wife, and we kissed. Damon held me so close, so close that I thought for the first time since I'd been with him that it was done. That we were one. That we'd be together forever, like this, two souls who were always meant to be together, who went through hell and back to get here. We would be together forever.

"I love you, Lina," he whispered in my ear.

"I love you."

The End

Keep reading for a sample from Zach Amado's story, Unhinged!

SAMPLE FROM UNHINGED
ZACH

Finding people who don't want to be found has always been one of my specialties. It's what got me into special ops.

It's also what got me killed.

Well, almost got me killed.

It isn't quite pitch black when I step out of my SUV and onto the street. *Her* street. The full moon shines bright overhead, making the clouds appear silvery, making them cast shadows as they skim past. I don't duck into those shadows, though. I take my time walking to her house. Don't bother hiding. I stroll, in fact—if a guy my size can stroll—right up to 13 Rattlesnake Valley Lane.

Her garden is small, but neat, not a single weed in the lush green grass. The walkway swept clean. Perfect. No cracks in the concrete. It's just like her, actually. Perfect—on the outside. The inside's where the damage is.

It's a warm night, even for Denver, but she has all the windows open. Sheer curtains blow gently, but the breeze is getting stronger. It carries a storm on its heels. An omen.

When I reach her door, I slip my key out of my pocket. I made a copy a few weeks ago. She hasn't noticed I've been coming and going for that long. But she's never been home for my visits. Not yet, at least. Not until tonight.

I turn the doorknob and open the front door. I know the exact point when it will creak, so I make sure I'm in before it does. I don't bother locking it behind me. Locks never keep those they intend to keep out, out. It's naïve to think otherwise.

By now, I've memorized the layout of the small house. It's another of my talents. I see everything, every single detail most people don't even notice. It's what saved my life the night I was meant to die.

The living room is picked up, and utterly impersonal. It's like no one lives here. I wonder if she rented the place furnished because it doesn't look like what I imagine she'd like. This stuff is all too big, too rustic. Too secondhand.

I almost nick my shin in the same spot I have twice before, but move just in time as I make my way toward her bedroom. She sleeps with the door open. I'm guessing it's for ventilation. I wonder why she doesn't run the AC, but maybe it's because of her background, where she's from. She's lived in the desert. Grown up in it. Maybe to her, this is cool.

As I get closer, I can see her soft, feminine shape lying beneath the single white sheet on the bed. She's on her side, face to the window. Long, dark hair is strewn across her pillow. She's got one arm over top of the sheet and I recognize the scar where a bullet skimmed her skin two years ago. She'd been that close to dying. If I hadn't tackled her to the ground when I had, she would have died.

And maybe six others would have lived because of it.

Stop.

I can't go there.

Not now.

Right now, I need answers.

A cloud crosses the moon, casting a shadow over her face as I approach. It's gone as quickly as it came though, and a moment later, I'm looking down at her, at Eve El-Amin. And even though I've been tailing her for weeks, memorizing every detail of her new life, being this close to her, it does something to me. Being near her has always been difficult, dangerous, but this time, it's more than that. Or at least it's different. It stirs up all those old emotions—anger the predominant one—but something else, too. Something dark and twisted inside me.

A thing that wants what it wants.

I close my eyes momentarily, quashing that last part. Shoving it deep down into my gut. It's no use. Not here. Not now. Because too much is at stake to let that side take over.

It's like asking the question of why. It's no use trying to understand why. Did she know that night was a trap? Did she know she was sending us into a massacre? Why would she do that? Why, when every single man who died that night would have laid down his life to protect hers?

I feel my chest tightening, along with my jaw, my fists. Eve mutters something in her sleep. I'm not worried she'll wake. My heart doesn't even skip a beat when she rolls onto her back. That's how far gone I am. That's how little I care if she does open her eyes and sees me standing in her bedroom, looming over her as she sleeps.

And that's what makes me dangerous. Makes this mission—my private vendetta—so fucking fragile.

I need to fucking care.

I need to get my head out of my ass and focus on why I'm here.

If she sees me now, it'll fuck up the grand entrance I have planned. For weeks, I've been going through her house. Drinking her liquor. Eating her food. Leaving empty containers on the kitchen counter. Moving her mail. Little shit that makes her think she's not paying attention or forgetting. Unnerving her. Making her look over her shoulder.

That little shit is changing tomorrow.

Tomorrow, shit gets real.

I look down at her face. She's pretty. Always was. She hasn't changed much in two years, which surprises me. I would have thought sending six men to their deaths would have taken its toll.

But then again, you'd have to have a conscience for that.

Her hair's longer. I bet the thick waves she used to tie in a ponytail reach the middle of her back. Her olive skin is pale for the time of year, still smooth, still perfect, just like her tiny nose, those lush, plump lips. I can see a little glimpse of white teeth behind those lying lips.

I crouch down. I'm so close, I can hear her breathe.

I inhale, taking in her scent, remembering it. Memorizing it. Filing it away as my cock stirs.

"Sleep well tonight, Eve El-Amin," I whisper, and I can't resist touching her, pushing a wisp of soft, jet black hair off her face. "Because come tomorrow, your days are numbered and sleep will become a thing of the past."

One-Click Unhinged Now!

Thank you for reading *Corruptible*. I hope you loved Damon and Lina's story and would consider leaving a review in the store where you purchased the books.

If you'd like to sign up for my newsletter and keep up to date on new books, sales and events, click here! I don't ever share your information and promise not to clog up your inbox.

Like my FB Author Page to keep updated on news and giveaways!

I have a FB Fan Group where I share exclusive teasers, giveaways and just fun stuff. Probably TMI :) It's called The Knight Spot. I'd love for you to join us! Just click here!

ALSO BY NATASHA KNIGHT

Unholy Union Duet

Unholy Union
Unholy Intent

Collateral Damage Duet

Collateral: an Arranged Marriage Mafia Romance
Damage: an Arranged Marriage Mafia Romance

Ties that Bind Duet

Mine

His

Dark Legacy Trilogy

Taken (Dark Legacy, Book 1)
Torn (Dark Legacy, Book 2)
Twisted (Dark Legacy, Book 3)

MacLeod Brothers

Devil's Bargain

Benedetti Mafia World

Salvatore: a Dark Mafia Romance

Dominic: a Dark Mafia Romance

Sergio: a Dark Mafia Romance

The Benedetti Brothers Box Set (Contains Salvatore, Dominic and Sergio)

Killian: a Dark Mafia Romance

Giovanni: a Dark Mafia Romance

The Amado Brothers

Dishonorable

Disgraced

Unhinged

Standalone Dark Romance

Descent

Deviant

Beautiful Liar

Retribution

Theirs To Take

Captive, Mine

Alpha

Given to the Savage

Taken by the Beast

Claimed by the Beast

Captive's Desire

Protective Custody

Amy's Strict Doctor

Taming Emma

Taming Megan

Taming Naia

Reclaiming Sophie

The Firefighter's Girl

Dangerous Defiance

Her Rogue Knight

Taught To Kneel

Tamed: the Roark Brothers Trilogy

ACKNOWLEDGMENTS

Cover Design by CT Cover Creations

Cover Image by Wander Aguiar

ABOUT THE AUTHOR

Natasha Knight is the *USA Today* Bestselling author of Romantic Suspense and Dark Romance Novels. She has sold over half a million books and is translated into six languages. She currently lives in The Netherlands with her husband and two daughters and when she's not writing, she's walking in the woods listening to a book, sitting in a corner reading or off exploring the world as often as she can get away.

Click here to sign up for Natasha's newsletter to receive new release news and updates!

Write Natasha here: natasha@natasha-knight.com

Natasha Knight

Printed in Great Britain
by Amazon